TRAPPED

BOOK # 1

ACHE FOR YOU

NANCY BEAUDET

Published by 4 Paws Games and Publishing
Humboldt, Saskatchewan, Canada

Attention: Permission C/O
Nancy Beaudet
204 50 McLean Street
Red Deer, Alberta. T4R 1W7

Trapped in Three Hill, Book # 1: Ache for You
Written and Created by Nancy Beaudet
Cover Art by Henry Buitrago
Edited by Matthew Kennedy
Formatted and Published by
4 Paws Games and Publishing
First Edition
Published February, 2016
ISBN 13: 978-0992030636
ISBN 10: 0992030633

Published by 4 Paws Games and Publishing
P.O. Box 444
Humboldt, Saskatchewan, Canada
S0K 2A0
http://**www.4-Paws-Games-and-Publishing.ca**

ACKNOWLEDGEMENTS

There are a lot of people I want to thank, people and places that made all of this worth it.

The first people I would like to acknowledge and thank are Vickianne and Kenn of **4 Paws Games and Publishing**. I know I've told you this a hundred times but you have helped me more than you could ever imagine. I have been submitting work to publishers for forever, only to get rejected. I've given up so many times and felt like every word I have written was worthless. I have kept writing because it's the only thing that makes me feel strong and powerful in moments of weakness. Even when nobody else agrees, my imagination is my happy place. You not only told me why "Ache for You" wasn't ready to be published, but you also went through it with me step by step and helped me make it ready to be publishing. This was the best thing I could ever imagine and it was just the help I needed. I have a really bad habit of finishing something, and backing the hell away from it. You allowed me to do this, but you always pulled me back towards in. Thank you for that.

I also want to thank my mother; she's been putting up with my random stories for years. She still believes I'm going to be a super-awesome best seller and I wish that maybe someday I'll get to be that for her. That would be super cool, or whatever. You know, whatever works.

I want to thank my husband Adam, for buying me a laptop when mine broke so I could keep writing, and supporting me in any way he can. He knows and understands that writing is all that I am.

For my father and my sister, my baby nieces, her husband, and my in-laws! Mark and Diane, you really are my second parents. For Luke, for being awesome. For my co-workers at Peavey Mart, my girls. You make me laugh every day and help me ogle over potential hot guy muses. What?! It's work! It's allowed! For Kayla and Sarah, my very own fan-girls. Also for Gabe for talking me out of distracting myself from seeing this project through. I love you all.

Thank you!

DEDICATION

For Neil, because every day we miss you.

"Grief does not change you, Hazel, it reveals you."

-John Green, *The Fault in Our Stars.*

"No guy is worth your life. Not ever."

- *Buffy The Vampire Slayer.*

CHAPTERS

Seven Years Ago

Waking Up Right in the Middle of It All - Cadence

I blacked out. I have no idea how; I couldn't remember pouring anything suspicious down my throat. Nothing other than my usual drink choice, a black cherry flavoured Vodka in a plastic bottle. I drank to drown my feelings out. I wanted to shut my brain down. I wanted to put myself on mute. It happened once or twice or ten-hundred times, I have no fucking clue.

I think that I lost count.

I was blind in a poorly lit room I was on a stranger's couch. The room was cold; I was pretty sure that it was dark out. I drove here alone, my first year of college was over now and I wanted one last hurrah before the rest of my life went down the tubes.

My bedazzled yellow bra was pushed up and my purple strapless dress was pulled down. A stranger had his hands on my legs, spreading me out. His rough and ragged nails scratched at my skin as he adjusted himself. He growled from the back of his throat. I tried to reach out to push him away but all I could do was flail. He had me in his control.

He wasn't small, this beast with his large body that took up half the couch. His blue jeans hurt my skin and his stomach was heavy against my bare navel. I could see just the smallest hint of his clothes. He was wearing a t-shirt, the loose neck full of holes. It was a darker blue, the knees of his jeans were torn and frayed, the denim tight around his ankles. He was wearing work boots. His face was a mystery shrouded in vomit though, he was the darkness and the evil.

I had always liked the colour purple and my dress was the perfect shade of wonderful. Plum Purple. That was part of the reason I had picked this outfit out, I had wanted to dye my hair purple the day I graduated from high school, but I was too scared to.

I had to be drunk to have the courage to dress like this out and about. The real me was scared of her own shadow. I wasn't myself right now; I hated that girl. The drunk me was obnoxious and loud. No one could tell me what to do, at least it had always been like that until now.

I puked, but it barely came up and out since the stranger wouldn't let me roll over. The evil darkness chuckled. I managed to turn my head, smearing vomit onto the uncomfortable couch. I moved my face up and down, marking both the fabric and myself.

I felt so gross. I wanted to hose myself down.

"Let me go." I tried to sound forceful but it came out as a garble. My throat was full of bile. I was disgusted with myself. My hands were pinned down. My arms felt like limp and loose, twisted backwards and numb to the world. I felt awful and terrible and all alone.

My fat legs must have been heavy because the darkness groaned as he tried to lift me and reposition himself. He told me that I should try some cardio, he thought that working out might help. He said that I was disgusting and gross. I wanted to tell him that those words meant the same thing, so he should think of better insults.

I wanted to tell him to go fuck himself but every time that I tried to speak, I just choked. Every time he chuckled I felt my insides twist with the invasion of poison into my world.

His hands were cold, his palms clammy as he ran his fingers up and down every part of me that was now up for show. His touch inside of my mouth felt how I imagined a snake's tongue would feel: slimy and cold. He kissed me hard, bruising my lips with his own. It was like he was trying to eat my face whole. I felt my body tremble.

The darkness took this as invitation when really it was a reaction to his evil. I opened my eyes and saw the darkness smile. He released my mouth and the sound of us detaching was something like an overworked vacuum. He sucked all the goodness out. I was left empty and used. I felt so ill. He didn't do anything well.

"Let me go."

"No." He leaned down.

His breath on my neck made me want to roll away from this fresh hell, but fat his arms had me caged in without free will.

"If I let you go you'll think that you can just get drunk and lead me on without punishment. That's simply not allowed Caddie Doll. I want what you were offering a couple hours ago."

Everyone that I had ever known called me Caddie Doll, including my parents and all of my so-called friends from school.

My attacker using this nickname for me was not a tell, it gave me no clues to who he was. None at all.

I started to wonder in the back of my brain if there was a part of me that didn't really want to know. What would happen if I could give a name to this evil? Would they help me? I doubted so. Even if I could tell anybody, I knew that they would only look at me and see a girl who had regretted unlocking her knees so easily. No one would believe me.

"No," my voice was not loud. I felt feeble and small. I had never felt small. I was a big girl. I had always been a big girl. My hips were round and my back had its fair share of fat rolls. I wasn't beautiful. I wasn't delicate. I was never weak.

I did not need to be protected. I protected myself.

My long hair was a dark chocolate brown, it no longer felt soft against my knuckles. The strands were soaked with alcohol and stomach acid. I hadn't eaten in a while. I had nothing left to puke and yet I puked on him again anyhow. He growled.

I was only twenty years old. I still felt like a child. I definitely wasn't an adult. I lived on my own and almost always spent the night out and about. Perched on bar stools downtown glancing around, an insignificant mound of girl in a garbage pile so desperate to drown.

Three Hill was a small town. It was home. It had always been my home. I tried to blend into the crowd in middle school, and even high school, but had universally failed to do so. I was quiet and I was loud, I was awkward as all hell. No one wanted me around. Then or now.

I could hardly blame them, though. I tried for years to like myself, because everyone always said that the only way for others to love you was if you first loved yourself. I used to watch a lot of daytime talk shows.

I tried so hard to find something about me that was worth hanging onto. My searches came up empty. I liked my crooked smile, but my stupid snort whenever I laughed ruined the allure. I was ugly, people told me this all the time growing up. I was annoying, I legit road the short bus to school. I was that girl; I was special in the cruellest way possible. I clutched at nothing but alcohol; my demons were always so damn loud.

Drinking tuned it all out.

I heard my phone.

I heard the stupid ring tone I had recorded off of my CD player at home. I felt hope. My heart hammered in my chest, my eyes, which had refused to close, burned now. I tried to turn my head to look around. Oh Alex! That was his ringtone. He would call. My baby brother was only sixteen years old. He knew me better than anybody else. He would help. He wouldn't let me down. He would save me somehow.

"Please let me go. I promise that I won't tell," I angled my face away from the greasy lips attacking my face and the mouth that smelled like asshole.

"Too late for that Caddie Doll." The creep grabbed my boob, curving himself on top of me before pinching my nipple.

I yelped.

"Let. Me. Go." I found the strength to jolt my legs up into his groin muscles. The big galoot barely moved. I reached a hand out, feeling for my phone. Were other people in this darkened room? I couldn't tell. I could hear strange sounds.

I wanted to ask the ghosts about their obvious lack of morals, astounded at the lack of help. I wanted to be rescued. This weirded me out. My fingertips connected with the hard plastic of my pink Nokia flip phone, but before I stretched my arm further out the darkness on top of me had suddenly moved. The darkness was gone. Lifted off of me by some sort of miracle. A miracle that had muscles.

That asshole on top of me was huge. He was gone now.

I could breathe. I gulped heavy oxygen down.

I heard the sounds of flesh being pounded by furious fists. I rolled over onto my hip, pulling my knees up as I choked. I tried to cover myself, feeling for my underwear but they were somewhere on the ground.

I sat up a little.

"Here," a voice said, somewhere close. I heard a body being dropped rudely against the soft carpeted ground. "What a douche," the soft voice mumbled. I tried to look around but all I saw was a shadow. The voice handed me someone's coat.

"Come on, you need this more than I do."

I took it, nodding.

"Thank...thank you." I could barely get the words out. When I opened my mouth a chunk of something gross fell out. Oh no. My eyes locked on the shadow. He turned around. Holy unicorn angels.

Even in the shadows my saviour was beautiful. He held himself strong and tall, his hands tight against his sides. He was younger than me, I could tell. Still, I couldn't help but enjoy the shadowed view.

"It's fine. You don't need to thank me or anything, just cover yourself with that, you should be okay once you pull your dress down. I'll help you out. I think your brother's van just mowed the mail box down. He's freaking the fuck out." My saviour sounded strangely proud, again he smiled. He was looking around as he laughed softly to himself, rubbing at his jaw. How was anything funny right now? I wanted to shout before I got mad at myself. Realization turning into soft doubt.

Alex was here?

Why? And how?

I never got to answer my phone. I sat all the way up. Pulling on the coat and fixing my dress so that my boobs were no longer hanging out.

"You shouldn't drink so much." My hero rattled, it was only then that I noticed how nice his voice really was. It was soft and showing of his youth. I could tell that we separated by a few years or so.

"Something really bad could have happened to you."

"Yeah," I mumbled, "Says who?"

"Me." He finally got really close to where I sat on the couch, locking sharp green eyes onto my dull brown. "My name is Mal."

Now

1 Waking Up Right in the Middle of It All - Mal

It's like having your soul ripped out. The most important part of you just simply removed, over and out. Your body has been left with a gaping hole, and you have no idea what in the hell to do. It feels terrible.

I can't go on without you Pretty Girl.

I won't. It's just not fucking possible; it would be cruel. I have no idea how to breathe without you. My chest is heavy, and my heart is full. This weight in my lungs is one that I can't get used to.

I could scream, but I feel as if I won't make a sound. I feel as if I am buried underground, on fire in the pits of hell and yet frozen to the bone. Even if I could be heard, I don't think that it would truly matter anyhow. My voice is meaningless sound. No one is listening right now.

It's not like I've always had a never ending list of people that I can talk to, I only ever had you. Only ever you.

As an asshole who also happens to be a twenty-one-year-old dude, the friends I make are far and few. I never trusted anyone but you. Not really anyhow. Not deep down. I don't know how to trust people.

When I open my mouth, my secrets don't just spill out. That only happened when I was talking to you.

You had this way of looking at me, even when looking at you made me want to pull my teeth out. You just looked at me and I knew, no matter what I told you. I knew that you would never bolt.

You would never leave me alone.

You left me alone now.

The gravestone that your mother picked out does nothing for you. It's simple grey stone. Your name is carved out along with a bunch of words and some touching quote. Flowers and mementos litter the freshly green ground, small hand-held teddy bears wearing pink tutus. I know that if you were around still, you would throw it all out.

I don't care to look at any of it right now.

I think that fancier people would call the stone marble. I won't. I spend my Saturday nights alone eating fast food and reading spy novels. I'm not a fancy kind of dude.

The peace garden that has become your home still gives me the chills, even though the September sun is warm as it beats down. I urge the green grass to turn brown. Everything else has started to. It's all sorts of beautiful out right now. Our hot summer is turning into a breezy fall.

Everything around me is framed in orange-gold, the trees are crisp and turning dead and cold. They stand lean and tall hundreds of yards from where I crouch down. The breath I breathe is ice cold.

The sun is making me sway a little. It rained all night.

I can tell. When I woke up there were water remnants on my windshield. I parked my Camaro™ and walked to your headstone.

I didn't even think that leaving you here to decompose was legal, no one in town made a big deal out of it, though.

This is not a graveyard.

This is a public place, perfect for an evening stroll. A peace garden if you will. I'm pretty sure that that is what it is officially called. There's a huge metal sign hanging above the parking lot. It curves and the letters are dead and beautiful, burned out of black metal.

You are all alone.

I wanted to say something to the people who buried you, like why not just leave her behind a funeral home? It's probably just as illegal.

What about the buffet downtown? They have nice dumpsters, big and small. All in a row.

Leaving you there would be just as tasteless and cruel, if not more so. But I kept my hand over my mouth because there was no use in upsetting your parents, as they had already been dealt a fatal blow the moment that they lost you.

I'm still shocked at the selfishness of you.

I look around, wiping tears away from my nose. How long have you officially been gone now? A month, or is it two?

I have almost completely lost the ability to count.

I dread the day that I will need my fingers and toes to figure out how long it's been since you left town.

The days blurred together, weeks became meaningless and the minutes and seconds became meaningful. I numbed myself. I needed to.

I've lived in the same small, shitty town since I was in preschool. I was born here after being conceived in a crappy hotel and I will someday be buried in the cold, wet ground that surrounds me now. I refuse to rest in peace away from you.

Perhaps that day will be soon?

Yeah, that would be so cool.

Everyone wants out of Three Hill. To an outsider it all looks beautiful. To someone not in the know.

There is only one way in and one way out, trees line every road and every road leads back downtown. Every building and every house was built over a century ago. Every shop is built out of red brick with apartments overhead that mostly remain unused. They are almost all identical.

They all look out onto streets of gleeful, glowing people. Liars who are only visible through large bay windows. I hate this town. I hate these people. I only liked you.

I starting calling you Flo because when I looked at you I didn't see a girl named Ruth. I saw someone beautiful. I saw someone cruel and unusual and someone who would happily steal everything that I had come to know.

I wipe my palms off on my sweat pants. I'm clammy and uncomfortable. I'm not dressed for the weather at all. My yellow jersey is just something I found inside of my couch. It's sleeveless and could stand to be washed a time or two. I'm wearing socks with sandals.

My black hair is slicked back with grease, not hair gel. I did try to spike it up a little, though. Just for you. I haven't showered in a while. I'm pretty sure that I'm starting to smell.

I look down at you and force a smile. I wonder what on earth you would be doing right now. You were only nineteen years old.

Now you are immortal.

I guess dying young will do that you.

I can't even look at pictures of you now, doing so makes me feel ill. I retreat from every inch of proof that you were real and yet I cling to it with everything that I know.

I sit down, dropping my ass against the damp ground. I rest my forearms on my knees and rock back on my heels, glancing around.

Since it's early there aren't a lot of people hanging around, but there are a few. Just no massive crowds. The park isn't within walking distance of the college but it does sit as the backyard of a fish and chips restaurant and a dollar store. A strip mall where homeless people like to hang out, this is one of the seedier parts of town, even though we're on the outskirts of Three Hill, nearest to highway and far from downtown.

I wanted better for you.

I wanted more for you.

I pick at a scab on my left knuckle, looking over at the lake and the boats that have been tied against the dock.

No one is on the beach, but there are a few people on the walking trails. There are women in halter tops with sports bras plainly visible, yoga pants that leave nothing to the imagination at all. They're begging for attention only to complain about being ogled.

I already told you I was an asshole. You have no reason for being surprised now. I drop my back against the ground, stretching my arms and legs out. I make an imaginary snow angel when there isn't any wonderful snow. Looking up at the pretty blue sky, watching white clouds move. I know that they are probably not really moving at all but my eyes are playing tricks on me and I enjoy the show. I haven't been sleeping well. I haven't been sleeping at all. I'm worn out.

I'm surprised that I can still cry at all, I thought that I had completely run out of things to feel. Anger and denial.

I keep waiting for depression to follow. I think we've already become acquainted though. Depression and your good old buddy, old pal. I don't know. Maybe that is also denial. What happened to you? Why did you decide to go? Why didn't you text? Why didn't you call?

I fucking hate you some days Flo, and I don't even care if you can hear me right now. I don't care if my thoughts hurt you. You deserve to know how you made me feel. You deserve to be miserable, too.

I hear my name being called; it isn't enough to pull me out of my own dreary clouds. I can only blink, listening to the call as it echoes. Annoyance fuelling the speaker well.

I don't sit up or look around. A heavy breathing mammal appears next to my left elbow. It blocks the sun and leaves me in someone else's sweaty shadow, souring my mood even more, somehow. As if that was even possible. Doubtful.

I look up and get grossed out. Yeah, I'm a dick hole. The mountain smells like body odour and dick cheese rolled into a buffet. A buffet that's quickly running out of tables, the damp floor coated in mould and puke.

"Can I help you?" I mumble, lifting up my arm to shadow my face from the smell.

"You okay dude? You've been down there for a while." A voice carries straight down; the mammal has its elbows propped out. Hands on his hips. Legs widely spread. He's wearing gym shorts.

I can see directly up the gap of fabric making up his leg holes. I could probably see his tiny little dick if I concentrated, which I'm not about do since I'm not into men like that. Although, it would make for a pretty hilarious six second video for the internet.

"I'm fine. Thank you." My words are quipped, neutral.

"Are you sure?" The voice becomes quizzical.

I laugh out loud, causing the mountain of shadow to sigh and scowl. "Fuck off." I mumble to myself. The shadow doesn't move.

"Come on dude. It's me, Michael. You remember don't you? We used to hang out a little in school."

Who?

"This look isn't good for you."

Michael? Who the hell is Michael? Since my brain is already scrambled, I have to squint to see through all the hoarded shadows. I've known a lot of random dudes and wow, I just realized how awful that sounds. I am not a male hooker, just so you know.

Let's continue.

I was enrolled in a lot sports when I was little, so I always had a friend hanging around my house. I played hockey well, I liked skating and body checking the other team. Which is probably why I got more penalties than anybody thought possible.

Oh yeah, I remember now. I met Michael in high school. He was a nice, big dude with a generous smile and long hairy legs that are almost touching my face now. He had kind blue eyes and a big, bushy beard if I remember correctly. The girls in high school all thought he was wonderful, he stood up for anyone who couldn't stand up for themselves. I personally always wondered if he was truly full of bull. No one is ever truly nice without something to gain.

I don't open my eyes against to the sun to see if I'm still correct on my assumption of what his face looks like now. I assume he is identical to what he looked like in high school.

"I'm not bothering you and if you don't like my look, I suggest you move on from gawking at the horror show. This is a public park but this isn't a public gravestone. I'm having alone time with my girl. Now move along asshole, no one asked you."

I only open my eyes enough to peer over at the standing mountain of so-called nice dude. "Fuck off, dude." Again I grumble, wishing that I could feel some sort of relief when Michael finally does as told, sighing to himself and muttering something pitiful.

I can't feel anything now, though. Can you? Can you even hear me at all? Where are you now? I know that you never believed in heaven and hell.

You were such a rebel child. Wild but always in control. You knew when someone was wrong without me ever having to tell you. You knew when not to trust people, and when to hold a helping hand out. You knew when someone else needed you. Only you, and no one else.

You knew when I was angry and when I wanted to be still and peaceful. You knew when I wanted to run for the moon. I wanted to run with you. I try to be invisible, and I eat everything with plastic utensils. I prefer to be wasteful. Leaving my gross and disgusting mark on the world, I learned the opposite of that from you.

I hate talking to people. I hate having to make small talk or pretending to be happy when I'm actually quite miserable.

I've been a straight fuck up since you've been gone. You're the dead one and yet it is my body has been left to rot. I am a missing person that the world forgot. Time moves on. I do not.

I dread getting up. I dread moving on because I can't risk the moment that I stop.

The moment that I breathe and my brain pretends that it forgot, the gloves come off, and once again I'm just a fuck up that one passes without a second thought. I am worthless and numb. I swallow the pain and invite it into my lungs. My stomach. I wretch it up and taste it all again.

Every moment, and I always end up stuck on the worst of what happened, because as friends we never got past it. You don't get to finish your story when the heroine is dead. There is no way for our story to ever end, you ruined it. You left me to take care of all of the finale arrangements. The explanations. I try so desperately to find a conclusion, but I'm distracted and full of procrastination.

I don't want to know how this story ends. I don't want to push past this one horrible moment. I don't want to stop rewording and deleting what happened because it is the last moment that I have left.

I see you in my face again, brown eyed, green haired and vibrant. A total bad ass. My every memory of you right now is perfect. You are in high definition, and I keep zooming in, loving the way that you smile, and your eyes soften as you take me in. You are an angel. Perfect. Innocent. Tasteless. Sarcastic. Cruel and mean as shit. I backtrack.

That's the shit that I miss. The sounds, the breaking glass and the touches you can't take back. How could you do this?

How could you bolt before the movie ends when you have already paid for your ticket? I never thought you would do this. Your light was infinite. Your eyes never ending with a hidden sadness.

I didn't get it. You never gave me the chance. You assumed I would be the bad guy and say as you predicted. Did you think that I would just tell you to "Get over it?" What kind of a friend would do that? What kind of a friend do you think I am? What kind of a man? I would have saved you in a minute. Faster than even that. Why couldn't you just let me do that? Let me have it. That's the moment that I most want back. The tension and the distance I never wanted to begin with. The awkwardness. All of it. The lies and the bullshit. Your sad excuses. Your voice.

The fucking sound of your voice. I can't hear it now, and I don't want to be able to. The memory wouldn't do you justice. I know. It would be a sad and pathetic copycat. Not even an echo. Fuck I miss you.

Can you just come back now? Resurrect yourself and crawl out of the dirty ground? I promise that I won't hold what happened against you. I won't even mention it for a good month or so.

Seriously, though, can you just come back now?

2 Waking Up in the Middle of It All - Flo

What am I supposed to say? No, I can't just come back right now Mal. Death is kind of permanent; you know? I fucked myself over. I am royally screwed. I no longer get to be the storyteller of my own tale. Now it gets to be told by someone else. Whatever girl you meet who is kind enough to draw your heart out and make you feel. I don't want that to happen, just so you know; I never wanted it to happen. I wanted you all to myself.

I'm still a selfish asshole.

I'm scoring 152 on the creep scale right now. I'm busy leering at you and watching your smile fall. I'm falling in love with your frown. Did you know that I was in love with you?

I never told you. I couldn't tell you. That would have gone against everything that we had worked so hard to hold.

Our friendship was made of gold. I would text you and you would call. You lie down and I remain standing still. I watch your skin fight back against the chill. I hate this bloody peace garden more than you will ever know. The soft wind whistles against my skin and bones. You have no idea how much I miss the way that your golden skin used to glow.

My palms are in fists for you. I'm angry at myself. I'm angry at you.

I'm wearing the same clothes I was wearing when I left town: black skinny jeans full of holes and a long sleeved shirt with seagulls all over the front of it. I needed to be inconspicuous. I bought a fresh bag of clothes and I left my Old beater at the mall because it guzzled gas better than you could guzzle down a bag of cheesy balls. I loved that about you, the fact that you could be a slob one second a male model the next, but like everything else that I had come to know quite well, I had to let it go.

I had to let you go. I suck at goodbyes though, so I didn't let us have any at all. It was just too painful.

I rented a Honda™. It was white and I think it was a newer model. I didn't really care about the finer details to tell you the truth. I just wanted out. I almost chickened out. I felt like a hideous troll almost as much then as I do now. I dyed my dark hair seaweed green a couple of months ago. All because of you, everything in my world is because of you.

Mal, my old buddy.

My old pal.

What happened to you? You look like hell.

Your silky black hair is all sorts of askew and you're dressed like some sort of piss-stained old dude. Your yellow jersey is stained with the aforementioned cheesy balls. A top that goes perfectly well with the black sweat pants that cling for desperation at your ankles.

Socks and sandals are never a good look, Mal. Not even for a man as beautiful as you.

I stroll closer to you, hands in the front pockets of my jeans. Glancing around, there is no one else here that I know.

Hundreds of people attended my funeral as a mock show of love and support that my parents fell for, and continue to fall for. They cried over my casket, which was over course, tastefully closed.

They refused to bury me in a normal cemetery with other dead and careless assholes I could have an afterlife full of strange ghosts and the midnight ghouls but instead, I only have you.

I have only ever had you. Does that make me sound ungrateful? I'm not, just so you know. You were never worried about me, or concerned with protecting me because you thought I was the bravest woman that you had ever known. That's what you always said, and I never believed you. I still don't. You thought that I could take on the entire world; I could barely take on you. Is that what you want Mal? The truth?

Oh crap, someone is coming now. A dude I don't know. He stops right next to you. He's tall with a beard and bright eyes that scowl. I roll my eyes at the clouds as the two of you start to exchange insults.

"He's just trying to help you." I shout even though I have no way of knowing if this guy is really trying to do so. Crossing my arms and twirling around, I pretend that I'm in a super-cool music video. I dance by myself to the sound of you laughing out loud at yourself.

I pretend that this isn't real. I pretend that I'm asleep, or just plain freaking out. This cannot be real and yet it is–quite painfully so.

Three Hill is more than a one horse town. I watch men strolling around in business suits, holding briefcases baring gold plated initials.

A lot of people use these walking trails.

I never noticed before now, I turn around. The suits the men are wearing are deep brown, totally crisp and professional.

"Geffen's knows his time is limited when it comes to this case file. It won't take long and I wouldn't be surprised if by the end of the week we have him blown out," says suit number one. Suit number two chuckles and the two men continue on their way.

I close in on the first of the tall trees now, shading a large building meant to serve as a washroom and change room for those venturing out onto the lake itself. I look around: no one is in a swimsuit.

People are sitting on picnic tables, wearing dark jeans and all the layers needed to keep a warm-blooded person from getting cold.

I walk further away, secluding myself. I reach my hand out to grace a low-hanging tree branch but I can't feel it, even if I touch it. My fingers just touch oxygen being sucked in the opposite direction. I keep trying but I'm never quite tall enough to reach it.

I push my green hair back; the wind moves it annoyingly against my skin. How can I still feel that?

I don't understand.

It makes no sense.

I turn back to look my best friend, the former reason for my existence.

I truly believed that. Mal is the only person who has ever made me regret being such a bitch. He's still on the ground, the only difference is now he has once again been completely abandoned.

"You can't hear me and you're not supposed to know that I can hear you." I mumble, moving nice and slow. I drag my ankles. I want to make as much noise as bloody possible. These flip-flops are so uncomfortable.

I speak to Mal. "I can feel your laughter and your smile, even though I don't see any trace of it now. You are a ghost. I can feel you touching my waist and waiting for me to turn around. You were always right behind me, no matter where we were or what we had gotten up to, at school, at the mall. You were always there when I turned around. You had an intoxicating presence about you that I crave now. Even when we were fighting, I was laughing, I'm laughing now. How is that possible? How do you make me so happy and so bloody miserable?"

I'm empty without you.

"I don't know how I got here to tell you the truth. I just kind of wonder around aimlessly now."

I am bored as all hell.

I kneel down beside you.

"I've been following you since the news broke; I have nowhere else to go. I can feel that stupid coat you left in your Chevy™ and I can smell your precious smell: man and engine oil. I don't know why you always smell like engine oil. I've never been able to figure that out. Is it your cologne?" I laugh out loud. The boy doesn't move.

"You have never been the best car guy in the world, but you were a great pal, weren't you? I'm supposed to gone now. I am gone now. I am dead. I am cold. I should allow myself to be only a memory, fading into the snow that is sure to fall soon, and not a ghost haunting you, stalking you and watching you. You've fooled yourself into believing that you are invisible somehow. You have never been invisible. Do you not see the way every female in town looks at you? You're a God damn tree dude. Totally made of muscles"

You are beautiful Mal.

You glow.

My voice breaks, I wish I could yell. "I said I'm sorry didn't I? For what went down. I said it in my head not out loud. There's hardly any point in me speaking now, you couldn't hear me anyhow. I'm a whisper, a ghost. I don't matter at all. I'm sorry for letting go. I regretted jumping before I even hit the ground. I wasn't going to hit the clouds. I know that sounds beyond stupid now, but jumping off of Buffalo falls was no easy feat you know? It took lady balls."

I breathe in and out. My words tremble "God, I am such a tool. I should have just got back into my car, called you and talked it out. But instead I had to take the scenic route through all that life-altering bullshit that morons like to spew. I had a choice. I chose not to feel because my feels had gotten overwhelmed."

I just couldn't control myself. Not around anybody else and especially not around you.

"I wanted to kiss you and hit you, and I wasn't allowed to do either and both would have introduced me to your girlfriend's new shoes."

"I can't even remember her name right now. She is not what or who I dream about. I did not kill myself because of you."

Don't even go down that route.

I won't let you.

"I was seriously ill, okay, Mal? Sick straight down to the bone. My insides were flipped inside out. I didn't just jump off a cliff so that I could stop thinking about you, I mean yeah I was pretty much down for anything that would stop me from missing you. I wanted to stop loving you."

I wanted to feel normal. I wanted to smile. I wanted to be able to breathe in and out without a weight crushing me down, holding me underwater. I was afraid to drown.

I killed myself because I didn't know how to talk my feelings out.

I felt like I was going crazy, with anger taking control of me and filling my body with rage. I didn't know that there was no undo button on mistakes this size.

The damage that I did to myself was not collateral, it was fatal. I'm sorry Mal. I am so sorry for leaving you and for not being woman enough just to talk to you and talk it through.

I fucking miss you, too, and no, I cannot just come back now. It doesn't work that way Mal. Anyhow. What the hell are you wearing right now? Seriously? What the hell is wrong with you? I can almost smell the man-stank coming off of you.

Would a shower kill you?

Ha, too soon?

Sorry, not sorry.

Whoa boy. Settle down. No need to kick my headstone! That's is some pricey marble you just scuffed up with your stupid sandals. You better be going back to school tomorrow! Hello? Mal?

Where are you going now?

Mal?

3 Fuck You Flo - Mal

I get up and kick some of the soft grass around. My body has made an indentation in the ground; I am my own angel.

I turn my back on your headstone.

I hate this god damn peace garden more that you will ever know. Why couldn't they just bury you in a normal graveyard? Huh?

Too boring for you Flo?

Ha, sorry girl. You know how much I like to bug you. If you can hear me right now, why not shoot me a sign? Fill up my gas tank or make my doors unlock all on their own. Do something useful.

Come on my Pretty Girl. Let me know that I still have you. I can't live without you.

I have my hands in my pockets and my head angled down when I hear a voice breaking into my world of dark and depressing shadows.

"Hey, Mal!" Some egghead shouts. I look up more out of boredom that anything else. Another dude is waving me down.

One earbud is hanging out.

Why can't people just leave me alone?

I didn't realize that people still used these running trails–the park yes, but the trails? Hell no, at least that's what I would have assumed (the girls in yoga pants don't count) but when I finally pull my head out of my ass long enough to look around. I notice that I was never really alone.

Not even a little bit.

Not even at all.

God, you should see River what's-his-nuts right now. Dude totally blew his hair out. It's fluffy and gold. He's tall but hardly built. Blindingly pale arms stick out under a blue t-shirt emblazoned with some sort of hipster band logo.

Normally I would laugh and tease you, Flo. I'd suggest that perhaps he got prettied up just for you. Guys always tried to go out with you, but I put a quick notice on every dick in town. Touching of my best friend Flo was simply not allowed. Did you know? God I so badly want to tease you. See the anger in your eyes. They lit up every time I bugged you.

I can't do that now. Fuck you.

"Hey, Mal. How are you?"

"I'm great. How are you?"

"Good. Look man," River continued, "I'm sorry about Flo. I know that sounds lame as all hell right now, but I just wanted to check in on you. I went to your mom's house. You weren't home, and she said she hadn't seen you in a while, like since the funeral? Asked me if you were cool."

River means well. I know. He has pretty blue eyes, the kind that you were always crazy about. I hated that about you, your tendency to fall for morons who would only hurt you.

You called River a douche canoe right before you left town. We were talking about something random, something completely unrelated to the dude that I am currently talking to. We were eating Chinese take-out and God I hated that smell. We were sitting in your car: The Old beater. The front seats were stained with I don't even want to know, but everything smelled just like you, your vanilla body oil, your discount perfume and that colour-preserving shampoo you stocked up on your bathroom shelf. It smelled like mangoes. Suffice to say, you had an odd smell.

We were parked in front of the mall. Listening to the radio, you knew all the words to every song on the top 40 countdown. I was amused by you. This memory means nothing to me without you here to feel it as well. It just spoils my mood.

I haven't smiled since you. Why start now?

"Mal?" River looks at me with a puppy dog eyes and sad, thin mouth. He's making the oddest expression right now, trying to draw me back into the real world.

I resist the urge to laugh out loud. The only person who could draw me back was you. This dude doesn't have a hope in hell.

"Yeah, sorry dude," I say, but I'm not sorry at all. "Yeah, I'm totally cool. Just you know, chilling out." I'm trying not to blame myself for my best friend in the entire world thinking that she needed to take the easy way out. "I've just been busy a lot, you know with school and what have you." I haven't been busy with school at all. I have all but dropped out.

The only reason I haven't made it official is because I need my student-housing-only townhouse.

It's small, but I paid the rent off with what was left of my student loan. I have nowhere else to go. I refuse to go home, no way in hell.

River believes my words at face value. As do most people.

"If you're not busy tonight a few of us guys are going out. We might hit up that new strippers they just opened downtown. I guess the whole inside is totally tricked out." River seems hopeful.

He's trying to make things between us cool by including me in his Tuesday night ritual of throwing change around. In all honesty, I wouldn't even include myself. I'm fucking miserable to be around. I open my mouth to offer a refusal, but nothing falls out.

I'm too exhausted to even groan or grumble.

I haven't slept since God knows when. It's not like I can't sleep without you; it's just every time I close my eyes I see your face in my mind. I'm far past that point of grieving every memory. I just see random memories and for a moment they make me happy. Silent moments of your time when for a good five minutes you were mine. Totally mine. Happiness flickers in my mind.

My chest is filled with a longing that won't fade. It aches and missing you comes in bone crushing waves. I spiral into misery and my next words come out acidic and burning.

"Why in the hell would I want to go to the strippers with a bunch of dudes? Most of whom I don't know," I smirk. Speaking super smooth. Cocky as all hell. You always liked that about me, Flo. I totally knew.

Don't go getting embarrassed now Pretty Girl.

River's face shrinks down a good size or two as he, like, totally cowers in on himself. Did he think that I was cool? Like cool with being spoken to and tracked down? Especially now? How is that even possible?

"I'm sorry bro-"

"No. I'm not your bro. No fucking way in hell. I'm an asshole you only spoke to because I was friends with a girl everyone knew. If anything I'm saying is wrong, go ahead, stop me now."

I dare River to back completely down.

He gulps.

I have an arm resting on the windshield of my sky blue Camaro™. I look around the park. The quiet sanctuary you now call your home. There are lots more women walking and jogging around that I didn't really see until just now, adding to the few I noticed when I first parked my car and got out. I wipe leftover tears away from my nose. Snot has dripped onto my lips, and I wipe at my mouth with the back of my knuckles.

I didn't even realize that I could still cry over you.

I'm surprised that the tears would even come out. I thought I had rung all the emotion out of my eyeballs by now. Oh well.

"You trusted me because of Flo. You stopped being afraid of me because of Flo, as did everyone else in this God forsaken town. Well guess what? She's gone now." I let the poor bastard know. I don't even have to try to insert death into my tone. It is all that I'm made of now.

I'm cold. I miss you.

Flo?

River backs up with his hands out.

I smirk.

He looks down.

"Like I said, dude, I'm sorry about what happened to Flo but I didn't stop being afraid of you just because you guys got close. I stopped being afraid of you because you stopped threatening to break my nose." This is true. "Anyhow, your mom was just worried about you."

Was she now? Couldn't take the time to call me herself?

River looks down at the ground, seeming to swallow something he doesn't want to be let out. He holds his arms out like a sparrow.

"See you around Mal," says the douche. I swallow the bitterness down. "Yeah, you too." I hop into my 1968 Camaro™. A Chevy™ that is super tricked out. The roof is down and I'm cold as hell but I don't care to pull it up right now. Fuck I wish that the passenger seat still smelled like you Pretty Girl, and I know how creepy that sounds, but you know leather.

Everything just washes out.

4 It's Not His Fault - Flo

Okay, no I do not know anything about leather you douche canoe.

Have you seen my car, Mal? That thing wouldn't know real leather if it chewed on the bumper while saying hello.

Yeah, I know that doesn't make any sense. Move right along will you? By the way, I'm in the backseat in case you didn't know. I chuckle and snort laughter, but of course you don't know. I'm fucking invisible. You can't feel me at all. I sat in the middle where there isn't a seat belt. Leaning forward so that I can watch your anger boil. I watch your knuckles turn white as you clench the steering wheel. The stereo is so loud.

Music always was your way of maintaining control.

"It's not his fault you know?" I watched River slowly turning around, watching you with more kindness than pity. He felt bad leaving you upset but I could tell that he had no idea of what else to do.

"He was just trying to help."

As are most people.

"He's a good guy, shy and a little odd every once in a while but still kind when it counts. I also never thought he was into me just so you know. That's not the kind of guy I attracted when I had a pulse, but still. It's not his fault. It's not anyone's fault aside from my own. I'm not going to blame you. I won't. That's not even in the realm of being possible."

No way in hell. I look out the back window when Mal turns around to reverse because I can't stand the thought of him looking right through me like I am not even here at all, which I'm not, but being reminded about it constantly still hurts like a bitch. I swallow. Mal parked his car between the lines for the first time since forever. He usually parks crooked. Like an asshole. God forbid anyone ding his vagina bait on wheels.

The minivan next to him is loaded with little girls in tutus. They all jump out without a care in the world. I could have sworn that one of the little girls made actual eye contact with me but my imagination always did have a tendency to run wild. Oh, well.

"We should stop for food, I'm actually starving. That's the funny thing about being dead. You stop feeling human and start feeling like some sort of alien but your stomach doesn't quite get it."

I rest my arms across my abdomen, sitting back. Mal pulls up to the exit of the parking lot and signals left, eyeing the right-hand side of the exit for any oncoming traffic. My stomach feels flat, as if nothing works inside of it. My organs have failed me by now I know.

I actually miss getting my period. How sad is that? I miss cramps. I miss the having a reason or an excuse for being a sudden and or constant pain in the ass.

"I doubt that you miss my PMS," I laugh, looking towards the back of Mal's head.

I want to reach out and touch him, but I resist. If he pulled away from my hand I wouldn't be able to stand it if he sank back into it I would be beyond ecstatic–if that level of emotion even exists once you're dead. I kind of doubt it. "Close the window man, you're going to get sick," I nag him.

His arms are full of delicious definition. His muscles twist and bend with the fury that rages inside of him. I've only ever once had the gift of seeing him shirtless. I try to bring up the image, but the memory is faded. I want it back again. I have always been jealous of his natural tan. His green eyes vibrant against his darker, golden flesh. Even when he's sad, he stops my dead heart in its tracks.

Mal is gorgeous. He always has been. It seems effortless for him.

He's so tense. I ache with how much I miss him. It makes me ashamed, makes me feel like an idiot. I hate being pathetic. I wish that I had super powers right now, something besides the ability to watch over you. I want to protect you. I want to pull my knees up against my nose and draw on one of the back windows.

I try to make a sound.

I want to yell.

I feel smothered right now. I look down at my black skinny jeans and pick at the ragged holes, revealing flesh bruised over bone.

"I wanted to tell you..." it feels horrible to say the words out loud, "I wanted to call you, and I wanted you to call me first without me having to ask you or lure you with my super unattractive and clingy pull. I just wanted you Mal, and I don't know what to do. I woke up all alone on the filthy blood covered ground and I don't know what to do know." This is the honest truth.

I touched you once. It feels like a hundred years ago now. I kissed you in super slow-mo. It was so good I never wanted to let go. You need to let go now. I don't want to let you.

This is horrible.

"Come on Mal, close the God damn window. This car is going to be full of mosquitoes and I may be dead and cold, but I'm still full of delicious blood cells. Those little vampires will love it. And turn the heat on. Like now, please and thank you. I don't want to be a vampire meal. Ha, wouldn't it be awesome if that song came on the radio right now?"

I wrinkle my nose. Quoting the the song to my favourite show, the one about teenaged vampires in high school. I always loved that show. Admit it Mal, you did too.

We binge watched that show.

"Come on Mr. Radio. Listen to me and make all of my dreams come true, play **Vampire Meal** and freak Mal out! Come on, do it now!"

I get super close, totally in his personal bubble. He's still driving, unamused and glaring out the windshield.

Ha. It totally worked. Oh, you're an oblivious boy. At least I amuse myself. Mal parks in front of his townhouse, right in front of a bench dedicated to some dead rich dude. Large trees line the parking lot and the sidewalk in front of it. A weeping willow cries gold.

Every student housing townhouse is identical from the inside out. I know because I looked at a brochure once upon a time, a long time ago. They're small. The outside is painted a boringly dark tan shade that spreads like creme beneath beautiful white trimmed windows.

Mal starts to get out.

Watching him slam his door just for show makes me smile. Always a bad boy I tell yeah. I stay in the back of the *Chevy™*.

"You were built for this car you know?" The soft grey leather interior and a killer stereo that I helped him install.

"You haven't cut your hair since the funeral. Since *my* funeral. Thinking about it that way kills you know?" It makes this all the more real and surreal.

Ha. How is that even possible? I'm dead! A nineteen-year-old ghost with dark green hair and whisky coloured eyeballs.

I dyed my dark hair green on a joke. You thought I'd never go through with it, and I couldn't forgo myself the chance to wipe that smirk off of your handsome face. I wanted to make your eyes roll. I wanted to rock your world. I failed.

I was happy to come with you and leave behind the garden of peace and new souls. No joke, that's what it's called.

My parents thought that losing their teenage daughter to suicide was so bad that they had to hide my death as if it was not a fact. As if they could change my soul's direction.

I might not burn in hell for this but being stuck following Mal around sure is giving my ovaries a good work out.

God, I would climb that boy like a tree if Mother Nature or heaven would allow me to do so. What? I'm dead. I can think whatever I want now. Go screw yourself. Just don't screw Mal. I am the only one allowed to fantasize about that boy. No one else. Is that clear with you all? Good. Let's continue.

I climb out of vagina bait on wheels.

5 Drown It Out - Mal

I watch the door of my car open all by itself.

What the hell?

I turn around, keys still in hand. I was sure that I left both front windows rolled down but they're closed tightly now.

Again, what the hell?

"Is that you Pretty Girl?" I stiffen where I stand, I drop my arms to my sides and I suddenly feel cold. Sunshine is flaming against the front of my townhouse, but I can barely feel it at all.

I feel dead, alone, but angry most of all.

I've never been one to believe in ghosts.

I'm desperate now. I'm a fucking fool. I have been for a while now; I want the pain I feel to explode.

I want the entire world to know to how I feel. I want everyone to feel like they loved and they lost you. I want everyone to feel the pain that I feel now. I want everyone in the world to pay because I lost you. I have no one to blame but myself and that just isn't cool.

I want to blame you. Why are you not here for me to do so?

I want to join you. I turn around, inserting myself into the shadows. It didn't take me long to drive home. I raced myself most of the way, pressing the gas pedal down with my hands clutching at my steering wheel. I always remained at ten and two.

I had always been responsible but carefully not careful; I did not want to be bored with my world. I was never bored with you.

Did you understand that Flo? I mean, did it really sneak its way into your stubborn fucking skull? I doubt that it did somehow. I need to go to bed and chill out. I need my thoughts to stop freaking me the hell out. I don't care how it looks to anybody else.

I miss you. I stumble up my front steps, keeping my heads down on the cement. I feel drunk with death.

The complex where I live is almost always quiet. I know that any of the real partiers can't afford to pay the skyrocketing rent. It's ridiculous.

I pretty much pay $1100 a month to live in a one-bedroom townhouse without heat or any soundproofing.

The foundation is cracked; anyone could plainly see that. The cream coloured panelling wasn't done recently but the living room is pretty big. It has a step up into the kitchen that I trip on almost daily. But alas, it's a better alternative than living with my parents.

That is also beyond obvious. Two drunk idiots with money to burn and oh they are so willing to waste it. My mom is just too chicken shit to light the match. So she leaves that to my dad.

I unlock my front door and head in. The front door is solid. It would be seriously hard for anybody to break in without ending up bruised and broken. I think that's what I used to like so much about it. I felt safe in my prison. That's what this is. It isn't a home. It isn't my safe haven. This place is a hollow fortress.

I've never dusted.

I don't give a shit about appearance. Not anymore, I guess. I used to be that kind of prick. I was always showing off the latest threads if you want to call them that. I called them new shirts and new pants.

I liked attention. I have always liked it; I have always craved it but for all of the wrong reasons. I didn't care to be noticed. I cared to be hated. I liked when people were jealous. I liked when you were pissed off at my existence.

My front door enters into my living room, the dark hardwood floors creak with my entrance. I stand by my empty coffee table, looking in on my kitchen. The walls are painted a deep forest green. The floorboards dark hardwood. The kitchen counters a cool granite. I run my hand along the edge of it.

My brown couch is leather and I have a black leather lazy boy recliner. A flat screen television sits as the centre, though I haven't watched TV in forever. The news is just a depression shit-storm. Cartoons don't do it for me anymore.

I actually caught myself watching that mother and daughter drama you loved so much. It was delightfully intriguing. Or you know, it was good and whatever.

I pull of my shirt and toss it towards my washer and dryer. I'll take care of that mess later.

6 This Is Bullshit - Flo

I almost lose my shit when Mal starts taking off his clothes.

I know that makes me sound like some sort of brain-dead, sorority girl on a **Webflix** special. I'm not that girl though.

I'm Flo.

His body is a wonderland I want to make my home. He radiates warmth and love and everything that I have never really known. He makes me whole.

"You told me I was special and smart and beautiful. You told me everything that I ever wanted to hear and more so. You say you want to die and join me the underworld? That's not possible." I walk slow, carefully circling Mal.

I try desperately to keep my eyes away from his but it is a feat that proves to next to impossible. How is he so beautiful?

His shoulders curve with muscles that I didn't even know he had until right now. His stomach is hard as a brick wall; even from all the way across the room I can tell. Mal is tall, almost six-foot-two. His waist is narrow, a happily trail disappearing past his navel. A line of dark hair points down, making me feel like some super turned on, dead weirdo.

We never got the chance to truly see each other up close and personal. We always moved slowly and yet I felt as if were speeding up a dead end hill. There was no escape with Mal.

"I love you, Mal. I have always loved you. I fell in love with you when I was 12 years old. You were so cool and strong and built and I loved you. I could not even comprehend how much I loved you. The intensity of it made me ill. I couldn't go to school; I didn't want too. I didn't want to see you, I couldn't look at pictures of you and I couldn't hear about you. I couldn't listen to you or be in the same room with you without wanting to kill myself."

This is the ugly truth.

"Loving you made me hate you, it made me hate myself. Falling in love with you made me mean and it made me cruel. I stopped being merciful with people who had never deserved evil." I stand in front of Mal, if he could see me right now, or feel me at all, we would be nose to nose.

I stand on my tip toes.

"I love you, you stupid, selfish, brain-dead, douche canoe. I one-hundred-percent unequivocally love you. There is only one thing in this world that I still know to be true and that's that I can't live without you. I won't, it's just not fucking possible. It would be cruel."

Would it though?

I deserve this hell. I resist the urge to slap Mal. This is not his fault.

"What's going on with you? Why are you so intent on being the biggest asshole possible?" I stop, looking down. "Sorry, that was a little rude." I amend myself, watching as Mal circles the room. He's searching for something invisible.

"I don't know why I'm apologizing. It's not like you can hear me anyhow. Hey wait, what are you doing to your cell phone? That was the last good picture of us –NO! DON'T THROW IT AT THE WALL!"

Pieces of plastic and glass hit the ground. It's broken and useless now.

"Oh I am so going to kill you."

7 Can You Hear Me Now? - Mal

I toss my phone at the wall. I can't stand my ringtone. Did you forget that it was just a recording of you?

Saying hello? You were doing this stupid impression of that dirty parrot that they used to show off downtown. *Hello? Hello? How do you do? Can I help you? Hello? Baby wants to kiss you.*

I hate the sound now.

I hate the memory of your voice because I know that my memory wouldn't do you right at all. I hate thinking about you or seeing you and yet I live for those nightmares that leave me screaming at my bedroom walls. I hate you and I miss you. I love you. I don't know how to do both.

"I am so going to kill you!" someone echoes. For a brief second it sounds like you Pretty Girl but we all know that that isn't possible, my townhouse is tightly closed. I don't trust my neighbours enough to leave my windows open when I'm not home, but we both know that the walls are far from soundproof.

It could have been anyone.

Perhaps that Sawyer girl next door finally kicked her loser boyfriend out the front door. If so, I should make popcorn and go sit on my porch. Yes, I am that kind of neighbour. There are girls all over Three Hill, I've kissed half of them but I failed to tell any of them the truth. I know now that none of them are you, and none of them will ever look at me like you do. Did, not do. I hate having to remind myself of the fact that you're not coming home. Like ever, at all. I don't want to blame you, but right now I will. You should have let me save you.

I knew how to save you; you know?

8 What the Hell is Wrong with You? - Flo

"Did you know how to save me? Like really dude? I'm calling bullshit all over you. What were you going to go? Stand at the bottom of Buffalo Falls with your beautiful arms held wide out?"

I cross my arms, yelling loud. I want your neighbors to complain about you. I want you to get kicked out of this tomb you call home. You should have never moved out of your parents' house. They may not be the best parents in the word, God knows every trophy they ever made you win, they wanted just for themselves.

Still, I know that they loved you, deep down. I know that they still do.

"You should go home, being here? It's not good for you. It's not healthy to live alone and wallow. This isn't that mother and daughter show you were talking about, although that was one of my favourite episodes." I'm rambling now.

"Do you remember that time we stayed up watching late-night talk shows? We ordered in Chinese food and sat on my parents' couch. My parents trusted you enough to leave us alone. I don't know how to tell you the truth; your reputation is no secret in this town."

I want to sit down.

"You said that the best Chinese food was served at the mall, yeah that was probably true. We should have eaten in the food court like normal people. We could have eavesdropped on all of those old people. I never could figure out why all the old people in Three Hill like to hang out at the mall, why not go to **Monster Milkshakes**? They have a breakfast-all-day kind of menu."

Mal starts to pace and the hardwood floor creaks with his every move, my own footsteps are hallowing.

I'm cold.

"I want to die, Flo," you whisper to yourself, head hung low. Your beautiful glowing eyes are closed.

"No." I don't want you to continue as if you never heard me at all, but I know that you will anyhow. And you do.

"It hurts when I swallow and it hurts when I breathe in and it hurts to breathe out. My stomach is aching, I can't feel my own muscles move, and my entire body is full of pins and needles. I don't feel real."

"What?" your words make me stumble.

"How do you not feel real? Are you ill? Oh no, no no no. This is not allowed; this will not do. I won't let you do this Mal, I would say not over my dead body but that phrase is a little tired out, and also, way too literal for what we're going through right now."

You ignore me. I want to strangle you.

"I jumped off of a fucking cliff Mal, did you not see the nightly news report? Death is not beautiful! It does not solve your problems and it does not take you where you want to do. Go ahead, do your research Mal. What about Google™. Did you do an image search? Check it out. As soon as the news broke everyone in our tiny world knew that there was no saving Flo.

The fall didn't kill me though; it was the sharp rocks on the way down. I think I may have *actually* succeeded in poking an eye out. Isn't that what the adults always warned us about?"

Don't run with scissors Flo. You'll poke an eye out.

"I wasn't dead yet when I hit the bottom. I was unconscious and bleeding to death with a good half of my skull gone, but I still had a pulse. The paramedics checked. The firemen. They told everyone that my death was quick when it was, in fact, slow, that it was painless when it was, in fact, pain*ful*. That's what kindness gets you."

Bull and more bull.

I could see it in their eyes though. They felt horrible. A young girl decides to off herself and of course she regrets it before she even gets halfway down the hill. They had to make my parents comfortable.

I get it. I do.

My parents needed to chill. Now when they look at my old photos, I think they see some angel. As if I jumped and flew into the heavens when in reality I jumped face first into awfulness. It wasn't romantic or epic. I didn't enjoy any of it.

Mal looks up and I feel my dead heart stall, his green eyes are abnormally small. His hands are balled into fists, and he's clutching an old pillow.

Oh God no.

He's crying. Mal, tough, hot Mal is crying into a pillow, and I don't know what to do. My entire being just gives out. I can't explain how I fall I just do. My knees hit the ground, and suddenly I can't breathe in or out. I guess I don't need to breathe but still. Fuck.

I can't watch this boy be in pain right now. I can't. His pain is not allowed because it simply makes me hate myself more than I already do. I feel guilt. Blame. I feel like a moron. A tool. None of that compares to the emotions that flood my chest when Mal jumps off of the couch as I crumble towards the hard ground. His voice is catching when he says one word that ruins it all.

"Flo?" his voice echoes.

I would give anything to be alive right now.

I feel like I'm rocking back in forth, in the fetal position on the floor while I'm standing perfectly still. Forcefully breathing in and out when Mal looks to the space where I have cowered up down and around. His green eyes are huge. Wet with fresh dew.

"Flo?"

Oh hell no.

My real name is Ruth. Mal started calling me Flo because everything out of my mouth was like something he'd heard in a rap video. I almost shot chocolate milk out of my nose when he told me that though. It made no sense then, and it makes no sense now. We were twelve, and we've been friends since grade two. So different from how we are now.

I force myself to stand across from him in his living room. Mal. My buddy. My pal. Wouldn't it be cool if you could see me right now?

9 My Eyes Hurt from Looking at Pictures of You - Mal

Is that you Pretty Girl?

"Flo?" I call out. I heard a squeal. Like a dog that just had its tail stepped on by some random asshole. I felt the air move. My heart is burning in my chest as it tries to get out.

"Flo? Come on. I heard you. I didn't imagine that. It was real. Don't go getting shy on me now." I laugh a little.

I officially lost my mind a few months ago when they called me and told me they found you. You went missing on a day trip. You wanted to run away, and if you wanted attention from me, all you had to do was say something. Come on Flo. Say something now. Do something. I can feel you looking at me. That's a lie. I can't feel much of anything but the fire in my chest is still burning.

"Say something..."

What am I thinking? Talking to the empty air around me, looking at nothing. Looking for your face.

I will not go crazy. That's just not in me. I'll happily die before my mind starts to eat away at me. No way. I want to be of sound body and mind when I leave this place when I see you again one day. I will not let my misery murder me.

I drop my hands and walk away. I push back at the pain in my face, hoping to rub the tears away.

"You left. You fucking left me, Ruthie! Ruthie Jane! That's your real name. Your birth name. Did you hate it so much because you hated yourself? Why were you angry? I can't figure out for the life of me why you were so God damn angry!"

You had everything. You had a life. You had me. You had a choice and daylight and the sunshine and laughter and beauty. You had everything. You had me.

You tossed it all away. You broke me.

"How could you break me? You said you loved me. I read it in your diary a hundred-million times. I tore out my favourite page and kept it with me at all times. You said you loved me, and you couldn't even say goodbye. Why not text me? Call me? Do something!"

"Say something Flo, please. If you are here with me, please do something. Prove that you didn't leave me!" I will beg and plead. I will bloody God damn scream if you fucking find the need to hear me say such pathetic and whiny things.

I'll do anything.

10 This Isn't Real - Flo

"Hey, Mal." I shoot him an awkward wave and shy smile, breathing raging fire out. Seeing him like this has turned my body inside out. I am covered in boils. My legs feel like rubber. I want to wash my hair. My face feels red and greasy from my tears. Tears that continue to spill over, I always was kind of an ugly crier.

"Oh, Mal I would give anything to kiss you right now." This is an embarrassing truth. I kissed Mal more times than I can count. I know the shape of his mouth better than I know my own. He is my safety. My home.

Was. Not is. That's over now.

"Say something!" My soulmate shouts and I feel myself tremble. He wants proof that I'm still around somehow.

I know.

"God damn you're beautiful." I will only speak the truth. My chest becomes a crater full of doubt when Mal's eyes drop down. I step forward as he turns around, flinging himself back down on the couch.

Those four words made my mouth dry out. I cannot speak them aloud. I don't know how. I want the ground. I want to be cold. I don't want to move. I can't take this feeling. This weight. This guilt.

I change my mind. I want to rewind; I want to undo everything I've ever done in my short life. I didn't want to die. I don't want to die and yet I'm dead already.

"Please don't do this to me," Mal cries, and I am broken and weak. I am made of nothing and everything. He can't see me and he can't hear me. There is no point in me being. I am nothing. I am the worst of everything that one person can be. I am truly empty.

My best friend hates me. Taking my next step isn't easy. My legs are shaking, but I need Mal to be near me. "Mal please baby," I say, wiping my damp hands off on my jeans. I am shaking. I feel queasy.

"Baby I'm so sorry. I know that you can't hear me but if you ever do anything in this life please just try. Try to feel me. Try to understand that I'm here, waiting and listening." I kneel at his side, pushing his coffee table out of my way.

Mal's chest is heaving. He's gasping. Breathing does not come easily when you are dying. I reach out to touch him gently before pulling away. "I'm so sorry." I can say these words a thousand times a day and still I know that they will never lose the meaning. They will never be empty. Not with Mal. Not with me. This boy means everything to me.

"Look I know that nothing I can say will make your pain go away, and I'm not going to lie and say that I'm happy. If you hear me, you would know that I was only bullshitting. Bullshit isn't pretty, Mal. It's just fake. I wasn't thinking. I didn't think because I felt like I was too stupid to do anything. Everything I said or did only made me feel like I was getting it from every which way. No one ever agreed with me. You didn't even like to agree with me. I know I shouldn't have let that shit bother me, but I did, okay?"

I may be dead and worse looking, but I'm still me. This blood under my nails? It's made of me. Everything about me is the same. I'm still a freak, but I'm a miserable freak." I laugh at my own voice. I imagine Mal looking at me with pity. He has his arm over his face. Large hands clenched tightly. I want to calm his breathing.

"Say something Mal please. Speak? For me." I reach out again but this time I force myself not to pull away. His skin against my skin is a happy memory, a place of lust and teenaged anxiety. Hot and happy.

"Mal?" my hand brushes the air around his red and ragged, tear stained face. His warm breathing chills me. I'm close but still so far away.

I'm burning up from the inside. I'm dead and alive. I'm learning.

"Mal?' I'm about to touch Mal for the first time since I ran away and he just up and, *rolls away.*

11 Suicide - Mal

The days are pointless without you Flo. Fuck. I got up this morning and realized that I fell asleep on the couch.

My back is killing me. My shoulders ache as well, and my entire being swells with misery that won't let go. I ache for you.

I haven't bothered to clean my house in a while.

I don't see a point. No one has come in here in a good two months or so. No one sees my bedroom. You didn't while you were you were still around because I honestly just never bothered inviting you.

You could have just shown up one day.

That would have been cool. We could have hung out or had rough sex against the living room wall. That would have been cool too. I would give anything now just to taste you.

The making out we used to do isn't what I crave most of all now. I just want you Flo. Only you. Under me with your green hair fanned out across my pillow. I want to fuck you in my bedroom. I want to make love to you and leave your clothes in the hall.

I want a future and life with you. I want more than you gave me. I want to stop looking at my cell phone waiting for you to call. That's why I tossed it against the wall. The temptation to call your voice mail is too strong for me now. Texting you is futile. I just want you.

I strip on my way upstairs and flip on the hallway light. The bathroom is at the top of the stairs.

It's dark and gloomy in there. I rid my lower half of my boxers and toss them back down the stairs. I hope they land somewhere that I'll forget about it later. It would be super hilarious if I actually had company come over. I need to shower. I need to shave. I need to do all these normal things that I shouldn't have stopped doing in the first place.

My face doesn't look like my face when I stand in front of the bathroom mirror, fully prepared to shave. My green eyes look grey, and my cheeks are sunk in. My lips are heavy. I've been crying for days. My weaknesses are showing in all of the right and wrong ways.

You'd be so ashamed of me, and then you would laugh at me, this is almost the same thing. I try to picture you smiling. You stopped looking happy when you saw me. I should have asked you why. My imagination hates me. I assume the worst things. Were you repulsed by me? Why? Is that why you didn't give me a chance to chase the demons away?

Come on. Flo talk to me. Stop leaving me.

I cover my face in shaving cream, picking up the razor I stole from my mom's place. It's pink. It doesn't cut me. I also stole her shaving cream. I hate going to the store, I hate shopping.

I hate making small talk with the shy cashier. The bathroom fan is going crazy. I turned it on without realizing.

I think my house is silent, but my ears are humming. There is music in my mind. Music and noise.

I'm screaming on the inside. No headphones can block out my own screams. Believe me I've tried, a couple hundred times. It just keeps aching.

The urge to start bleeding hangs in front of me, like a wet rag I'm too grossed out to throw away. I don't want to touch the damn thing; it could have a disease. Doesn't that remind you of me?

Diseased?

I mean, I haven't had an STI or anything.

I'm clean, metaphorically speaking. I spread shaving cream over my jaw, slapping it to the sides of face. I start shaving.

12 Consumed - Flo

I stayed up all night. This shouldn't mean anything, the dead don't need sleep. At least, that's what the world makes you think.

I still need sleep.

I still *like* sleep.

I'm still lazy, and would much rather do nothing all day than do a hundred fun and exciting things.

I don't like people; I don't like talking or joining in on activates when nobody wants me around. This is why I preferred sleeping during the afternoons when I was supposed to be at school.

I stayed up all night, kneeling on the ground beside you. I spent all night watching you and loving you, my heart broke when your breathing finally evened out. You fell asleep on your couch.

I cried beside you. I cried like a pathetic, whiny ex-girlfriend who couldn't let go but was being forced too. I forced myself, I know.

I was never your girlfriend Mal. I sure as hell am not your ex now.

You woke up, looking around as you cursed yourself out. I backed up, pushing myself up using the coffee table. "Mal?" I whimper, smudging snot off of my face with my knuckles.

You look awful. You sound awful. Your voice is hateful. I cling to it in the shadows. I cling to you.

You peel off all of your clothes, and I see all of you. I've never seen all of you. We've kissed, we've groped. We never made it into a bedroom.

I don't know if I'm thankful for this now, or if I regret it more than you will ever know. You once told me that you wanted to watch me let go.

Did you?

I follow you into the shadows. You stumble up the stairs and I stay behind you, fully prepared to try to catch you if you fall.

Oh God, this is something that only a truly perverted bitch would do. I'm watching you shower Mal. I'm standing right behind you. I'm in your bathroom. That quick shave did nothing for you.

Come on.

Wipe the pain out of your eyes and let the crying go. Holding it in only looks worse on you.

My body hums when you turn around, and I look down south. I can't help it okay? I always wanted to jump you but to see you vulnerable awakens all sorts of emotions that I buried long ago.

I swallow and blush when you look me and up and down. In reality you are just looking at your bathroom wall. You can't see me at all. I am invisible, a ghost. I could probably touch you and make it real if I concentrated for a decade or two, at least if all those ghost movies were telling the truth. But I don't want to freak you out.

"Mal?" I reach out and slink back when you dead eye the shower curtain, kicking it out of the way as you turn the water on. It is hot and loud. The mirror is going to fog up even with the fan set to loud and annoying as all hell.

"So what do you think of the new iPhone? I would totally get one if I weren't dead and all." I try to chuckle but can't find the sound.

Mal steps over the tub and right away I follow.

This makes me worse somehow I know. Standing behind him when he tugs the shower curtain closed. Water hits my clothes, and I instantly feel relief when I am instantly soaked. I love knowing that I can still feel. That the water can still touch me. I don't know how that possible but I don't care right now. Mal turns around, fidgeting, unsure of himself and again I look south.

His ass is perfectly hardened and small. The back of his legs perfectly toned, his feet are huge.

God damn, Mal.

He dips his head under the hot waterfall and braces his arms against out the shower wall. I am so entranced by his muscles. He's like a god; a beautifully handsome soul that should never be in this much pain let alone any pain at all.

Suddenly it feels like there is too much space between or souls and yet not enough space at all. Not even close. Before I can think my next move through I reach out, breathing in water nice and shallow as my fingertips grace the back of his skull.

He shudders, but I know that's because of something besides what I'm doing right now. Something about the water or something else. Something I don't even know about. Something new.

"You can't feel this can you?" My fingers drop down. Touching the back of his neck. His shoulders. I trace the tip of my nail down his spine, stepping back a step or two because I'm overwhelmed.

I have my hands all over him now.

I am a real creepy perverted and horny ghost. Don't judge me! How dare you! Mal growls and suddenly my own legs almost knock me down. He turns around. His gaze is shooting for mine like an arrow. He has me in his strong hold, and suddenly I know that he can feel me because I can feel him too.

My hands are against his chest, and his hands and arms keep me in front of him. Pushing me back away the splash soaked shower wall. His nose touches my nose. Our lips are so close.

"Mal?" I say, but his face doesn't shift at all with the sound. I try again. "Mal?" My voice is choked. His arms cage me in like an animal. His green eyes are wild. Mal breathes in and breathes out. His entire body is vibrating my own before his arms drop, and he simply turns around.

His shoulders are tense, and my body is full of fuel. Right away I know.

“You felt that too, didn’t you?”

13 I Feel You - Mal

A spike of pain runs my heartbeat dull.

I stand in the shower for a moment or two, back against the waterfall. I felt Flo. Felt her cold hands against my chest. Finger nails are digging in to my flesh, seeking out my bones.

I saw her, and I don't know if it was in my memory or not at all. Her skin was breathing earth. Like dirt and summer and fall. I could almost taste her sweet mouth before my mind started to backpedal on itself.

That wasn't possible. I couldn't feel Flo. That wasn't real. Shaking my head and looking down I step out of the shower and reach for a damp towel. I haven't done laundry in a while.

I tie it around my hips and wipe steam away from my damaged reflection. I blink. I could be going crazy.

That would be cool. It would be something new. Mal, the golden boy, forced to chain himself against white padded walls.

My bathroom is small, so I don't have to take more than a step or two to get right out. I wait for a moment or two before heading back down the hall. Not bothering to turn back towards an empty shower expecting to find my soul. Something in there was comforting though and for half a second I felt even more alone.

I felt the turmoil, and I do not think that it was my own.

I need to get dressed. I should go to school. Pretend to care about the real world. It didn't stop when I lost Flo and I feel like that makes every other human undeniably shallow. Everyone should be highly aware of the pain flushing through my body and pushing at my skull. If I'm miserable, I want everyone else to be as well.

I swagger into the hall and down to my bedroom. It's small but dark. I always keep the curtains closed now.

The sunlight hurts my soul. Also, I'm an asshole, and I like to brood. I cannot brood amongst the sun's healthy glow.

I grab some grey underwear and drop my towel, tucking my junk away before grabbing for a pair of black jeans. Shirt? I have always been vain and shallow. My body is the result of working out and eating well. I look at it now and feel nothing but guilt. Did you feel bad about yourself because I was such an asshole? You always thought I was hot, and I am sure you would be drooling right now, Flo. But I know that me always liking the super skinny girls annoyed you.

You didn't always feel good about yourself and my being such a vain jackass was a sore spot for you.

I liked my body. I went by looks alone. You thought I was giving you a dig when I made a comment about someone eating too much junk food. That's not true. I would happily lick whip cream and cookie crumbs off of you. I loved you for you.

Did you secretly love me as well?

I pull on a hoodie and skip throwing on a shirt. I roll some pit stick under my arms and head downstairs. Two steps at a time.

The door to the bathroom has closed itself. Oh well. It's still empty in my living room. I didn't lock the door behind me last night, and I don't lock it now. Grabbing my car keys, I head out into the cold. It's grey out. I look up at the clouds before turning back around.

My eyes find my bedroom window. For a second the curtain is no longer closed and for a second I think I see you looking out. Brown eyes. Dark green hair. Sourpuss mouth. God, wouldn't that be cool? Wouldn't just make everything worthwhile?

I start to smile without meaning to. The odd feeling drags my mouth back down. I don't see you. That's not possible. I turn back around.

I don't need to drive. I live within walking distance of the actual college but walking right now would mean thinking and going over what may or may not have happened a few minutes ago. It would only give me time to feel bad about myself.

Do you remember the first time that we made out? Ha. Of course you do. You always were a dirty girl. It was so easy to make you smile. You could light up the entire world. All I had to do was touch you. Get you alone, it was so easy to get you under my control. Pinning you against a wall or corning you in your bedroom.

I miss kissing you. I miss getting that first taste of you when your whole body just went wild. It was like uncorking a champagne bottle. Everything about you just flooded right out. Your lies. Your truth.

I already knew everything about you, but I wanted to know more somehow. I wanted to meld your heart with my own.

You made me whole.

Driving does not chill me out. I hate everything on the radio. Every song and melody only reminds me of you.

How predictable.

I jam my finger into mute.

Silence is not solitude.

I was never alone with you. You remember that feeling don't you, Flo? See I know you do. You have to remember it because going through this alone simply isn't possible. I know you miss me too.

I can still feel you.

14 How Could You? - Flo

Of course, I miss you, too, Mal, I mean God! How stupid are you? Are you just fucking figuring this out?

I followed you. Of course, I followed you. I will always follow you. That's like my only job now. It is the only thing that I still know how to do without coming across like a total asshole.

I totally look like an insane person right now.

I'm still soaked. I ran away from this school. A good-old college dropout who couldn't even take three weeks of being bossed around and corrected in class. I don't like to listen.

You knew that, and yet you were the only one who looked disappointed when I showed up to tell you that I quit. I quit college, and I quit my classes. My heart wasn't in it.

You said that you understood that but still, you were against it.

"I want you to have a future kid," you said, and I screamed something rude at you for calling me *kid*. "If the teacher is saying that you're doing something wrong, fix it."

Mal's wise words of wisdom: fix it. Just like that.

As if I had any control of the situation. The prick teaching English told me to write, so I did. I wrote an essay that ended up being a column because my voice just flows like that. I can't help it.

Couldn't help it. Not can't. Once again not to point out the obvious, but I'm dead.

I can't write anymore because it's hard to turn on a laptop when you're dead. I don't know what happened to my laptop.

I don't want to think about any evidence of my heart and soul being neglected and or tossed into the trash.

Writing was my thing, is my thing. Fuck I can't get this past tense thing right. I'm still here aren't I? Still feeling and screaming and following you like a lost, love sick puppy.

Your classmates are staring. I guess the hot moody guy is a real sight to see. I can't stop looking, any other face is a mystery to me.

Mal looks terrifying. Strolling beneath beautiful trees, one foot in front of the other. His hands and arms are swinging. He walks like a machine.

I walk like a baby deer ready to be hunted and eaten alive. I keep ducking away from stray eyes that look right through me. My clothes are still dripping water, and I'm freezing. I walk close behind Mal, trying to absorb his body heat. It isn't working.

"Hey, Mal," a beautiful girl speaks up suddenly. Her bright eyes say everything, she's a busybody, blond haired, blue eyed and tiny. I envy the fact that she's wearing leggings where she can be seen by anybody. I can't even wear those things in front of my parents without cringing. Skin tight and revealing isn't my thing.

She's totally Mal's type: obviously pretty without loads of makeup and a smile that blinds, her cleavage on full display.

My body isn't wonderfully curvaceous or anything, I'm kind of scrawny and average looking. Boring.

My hips are wide and full of potential for child baring.

Mal always liked girls from a size zero or a size three. Even though he kissed me and touched me, I still kept waiting for me to leave me. I never believed that he could love me.

"Hey, Casey," Mal looks at the blonde with a dead gaze that kills me, well metaphorically speaking obviously.

Geeze. I roll my eyes.

"What you been doing?" Casey tucks her hands in the pocket of her red hoodie. It looks fuzzy and comfy. I cry a little on the inside. I miss shopping and being able to change. I miss sweat pants okay? Scratch that. I miss leggings. Oh God. I would kill for a pair of leggings.

"I've been busy," chuckles Mal, scratching at his face. That shave did nothing.

The three of us have stopped walking. I'm still stalking.

"Oh yeah?" Casey takes a sip of the coffee that I didn't realize she was holding. It smells somewhat minty. Suddenly I wonder what would be the harm in me doing something, I don't know, A little creepy?

"Yeah," Mal shrugs. He's only wearing a hoodie and the skin around his ears is getting red. He doesn't look angry, just annoyed.

Mal has never been overly friendly, he doesn't have to be. He's popular and good looking, girls fell into his arms easily. With girls like Casey he was usually just smooth enough to get his way.

He'd get what he wanted and leave. That was just his way. I stop listening to Casey because looking at her with jealously is a waste of time. She's already winning while I rot away in a garden across from a lake.

"Do you mind?" I ask while reaching and concentrating, aiming for her hot coffee. It feels like forever since I've eaten or had anything to drink. That is such a strange feeling. I'm not hungry, but my throat is dry from aching.

I'm polite about it anyway. Sort of I think. Slowly skimming my fingers along the lipstick stained lid, I'm right next to her. My elbow hits her chin. She doesn't feel it. She just keeps looking at him.

"I heard about your .... your friend. I saw the announcement in the paper. It sucks what happened." Casey's face looks genuinely sad. "Did she leave a note at least?"

She asks and that nagging guilt is back. I did this.

"Did she what?" My aching heart says. Mal's face is no longer a careful mask. His eyes blaze with death. Anger. Hurt. I did this.

The pain in Mal's voice, I did it. I caused it. I put it there, and I made a show out of it. I zoomed the camera in on his expression. Would having left a note or text have lessened this? I doubt it.

"What kind of question is that? Are you interested so that you'll be the first to know what it said? Do you want to write it online where everyone can like and comment on it?" Mal demands. Casey is silent. I realize her coffee is hot chocolate that smells deliciously like mint. I stop trying to steal it.

"It's not like that." Casey starts to defend, but Mal cuts her off by simply raising his hand. I doubt that she fears him. Mal has never been a very gentle man, but he's not one built of violence.

Still, Casey falls silent.

"Yes, it is." Mal's voice falls flat, and he just starts off. It takes me a minute to shake my head before I take off after him. Relentless when it comes to keeping an eye on him. Three Hill is peaceful looking from the outside in, completely perfect with burnt red trees and a mailman grinning behind every hedge. Everyone looks pleased with some mass secret. I was never good enough to be let in on it. For me, this place was a prison.

You were different. You always had the chance to be different, to be perfect. You had it, why did you try to destroy it?

"Mal come on slow down." I try to catch up. He just keeps his head down, his long legs moving faster than I will probably ever be able to go. "That girl didn't mean anything bad; she was just trying to talk to you."

"It's normal, my death was kind of wild and people want to know the details. That's understandable, but I'm sorry that I'm the reason that people are bothering you." This is totally the truth.

"Mal?" he doesn't even turn around. The side entrance to Three Hill community college is open, and Mal is an avalanche pushing through it.

The walls are all made of brick. The front entrance is massive, six doors spread out for going out and in. I was glad when I heard that he enrolled here as a student, but I was still confused by it. Mal never loved anything enough to stick to it. Girls or classes. Music or drawing.

He was so God damn good at making music. I used to watch him humming along creating a rhythm. He always had the lyrics just ready in his head, already full of passion. He stopped writing that first time that I kissed him, and I couldn't help but notice it. Did I kill something inside of him? Trying to smother him? All I wanted do was touch it. Feel it.

I wanted to experience it, and instead I killed it.

"Mal stop it!" Again I reach out for him, but I must not want to touch him because my grip on his sweatshirt just slips. He disappears down the hallway, and I'm alone again.

15 Not Yet - Mal

I last five minutes. Five minutes spent listening to some waste of skin in some fucking class that did not even pause as I walked in.

No one tried to stop me, so I sat in the back. I wish I had my backpack, at least then I could lean on it. My legs are shaking; my skin is damp. I'm clammy and uncomfortable and I hate it. The classroom has an auditorium style to it, high rows of chairs narrowing into a circle where the professor is meant to stand.

I get up with a grunt and turn with a twist, pushing open the heavy metal door. It slams behind me when I exit. I let it. I do not care if anyone is bothered or interrupted by it.

No one calls out demanding an explanation. No one gives a shit. At least I've learned that.

I storm along the walking path. Head down, rage blooming inside of my chest. No one bothers me again.

My ride is still parked right where I left it, in front of my townhouse. I don't know what moronic part of me expected this to be different. Why would it?

I am only haunted in my head.

My girl is gone, God dammit.

She's not coming back.

16 I Can't Do This - Flo

"Mal what the hell are you doing? I'm dead, and even I'm exhausted." I dropped into the passenger side of his Camaro™ and grunted at a sudden, unexpected difficulty in the situation.

I can *feel* him.

I can feel the seat I'm sitting in. The door handle was in my hand. I was suddenly unable just to shift my way through it. I had to open it.

"What the..." Mal says. Forest green eyes wide open. He looks over at me or where he has no idea that I currently am before shaking his head and revving the engine. I close my door and shrug at him.

"What? How else did you expect me to get in?"

He has no response to that, which would probably happen even if he could hear my stupid question. He backs out and merges into the parking lot's slow and meagre traffic.

"What happened to my car?" I ask him. "I mean, not my car, not the fabulous Old beater, but the car I was driving right before it happened. The one I rented, Do my parents think I stole it?" I didn't need their permission to rent it.

Mal gives me nothing. Nada. Not even a grin. He can't feel *this.* "It was a last minute decision to leave it where I parked it. I wanted to drive it over the edge like that badass movie where those two women did but meh. That seemed too dramatic. Plus, I only rented it. I didn't want to be responsible for the rental company having to pay for damages. They gave me a good deal, but I had to empty out my pockets to fill it full of gas. Damn gas guzzling piece of shit."

Mal signals left.

"My real car though. My Old beater? What happened to it? Do my parents still have it? I would be totally okay if you wanted to drive it. My mom would only wreck it. Plus, I left a bunch of personal shit in the back but I guess you already know that."

Who has it?

My shit? God, I hope it didn't all end up with my parents although I don't know why that wouldn't happen. Of course, it would go to them. When I ran I wasn't thinking about that. I was just looking for the next exit. I found it with a casual glance. I never intended for Buffalo Falls to be my final destination. I had never really believed in any of that.

Did Mal? I honestly never thought to ask.

Again he signals left, and I realize we're headed towards one of the many highway exits. He's headed right for it. I don't even know how to explain how I know this. I have to stop him. He doesn't want to see what I did. He can't. I won't let him.

"Mal come on man. Think about this. That place, I'm not in it. If you're looking for some sort of reasoning that death trap isn't going to help you see it. Trust me, I already went looking for it."

Reasoning with him may be a waste of breath but I'm up for it. Before anything else Mal is my friend. My best friend. I love him before I'm in love with him. I only want what's best for him.

"If you're listening Pretty Girl I need you to show me something," Mal suddenly says, gripping the steering wheel as he looks only at what's ahead of him. "I need you to show me what it looked like when you looked over the edge. Did it look like a requiem? Did the sunset make you see everything but sadness because honestly Pretty Girl? I don't get it. I don't know why you did what you did, and I can't stop thinking about it. If this is my end, then so be it because I can't handle this."

"Of course you can't." I cut in. "No one can handle death. No one human. That's what you are Mal. You're human, you feel everything, and you help people without them having to ask for it. You were a good kid, a good friend, and now you have the chance to be a good man. Don't do this, my friend, just don't do it." I don't know what happens, but suddenly I'm crying and reaching for his hand.

He flinches at the chill of my skin. God I really can feel him.

"Don't do this," I tell him. I do not beg or plead with him. I just simply tell him and believe that he has to listen. Even if he can't hear it.

Buffalo Falls isn't far from Three Hill. I ran and drove for hours and days only to come back. Months of being gone and the thought of Mal brought me right back. I wanted to feel close to him.

I missed him.

"Do you think that I don't regret it?" I whisper for him. "I regret everything about it, but I know enough to know that the only way I was going to realize how permanent death is, was by committing myself to hell with it. I was destined for damage Mal, you know that. No matter what I would give I know that I can't change what happened." My hand closes over his and I watch his fingers flex with the movement.

I'm not brave enough to look at his expression.

"Do you feel that?" I ask. I already know the answer is yes, but I would give my entire body and this moment to hear him say it.

"Yes," Mal says, and I am so sure that I imagined that, but it doesn't matter at this moment. I let go of him as he breathes in.

"Okay now stop being dramatic. I may already be dead, but I would appreciate it if you stopped trying to give me a heart attack. First the nakedness now this? Come on Mal. I'm only human." I tease him, "Let's head back. I can creep you out but somehow managing to have a bubble bath while you take a much needed nap."

I reach again to pat his hand. I'm halfway there when something glimmers up ahead, a sudden spark of madness. Suddenly I know that we've skipped to the end and missed a bundle of pages. There's a flash, and I blink to rid my mind of it. We are pulling over, and I feel like I'm being pulled into his lap. No. I've lost it. I imagine this only because of how badly I want it. His body is hard and welcomes me right in.

I scramble for a steady grasp.

Trying to blink my way out of this, whatever this is. It hurts, and I know that my brain is only playing tricks, but suddenly I am consumed with the possibility of it. I want to give in to my illusions.

I've snapped.

I'm somewhat okay with that God dammit.

Mal's voice breaks with three words–one sentence –followed by a soft and easy laugh. I feel my entire chest collapse.

"You came back."

17 Tastes Like Sex - Flo

His hands are on my lower back. I have my hands against his chest, and suddenly I am looking everywhere but directly at him.

Mal.

My buddy.

My friend.

My eyes burn with a faded recognition.

He's real, I can feel him. It feels like forever since I touched him. I told him that I loved him. Even if he didn't hear it I'm embarrassed. My body feels feverish but my skin is like ice when it touches his.

"You came back." He says it again as if the first time didn't quite stick, as if somehow I didn't quite hear him. That would be ridiculous seeing as I'm sitting right on top of him.

I'm in his lap. What. The. Frack. My lips just barely brush his, like an almost-kiss, despite the fact that his hands have moved to the back of my head and are trying to fuse my face against his. His eyes are closed but I just can't stop gaping at him. Mal just seems drunk with all of this. Drinking it in.

I can't get away from him. I need to stop him.

"I knew that you didn't mean it," Mal says. "I knew that you'd come back if I tried to make you mad." He laughs a soft laugh that is almost enough to do me right in.

Every part of me is almost touching him. As if I'm only here for a millisecond. This kiss could be real if we both wanted it. Perhaps.

Or it was never real to begin with. I do not want to give too much thought to the possibility of that.

"Yeah I'm so not doing this." I grip his sweatshirt in my fists and start to push off of him. The steering wheel is digging me in the back. All I can almost feel is the pressure of Mal's hands. It's like we're dancing.

Like magnets, the push and pull force me back from opening my mouth to kiss him back. I'm exhausted. Touching him and not slipping right through him takes a lot of concentration.

"Not doing what?" an intoxicated Mal asks as his lips find my neck. My ears, my eyelids. One hand clutching at the back of my head, the other curving over my ass. I'm still in his lap. Straddling him.

I can't take this.

I kiss him back. Opening my mouth to let his eagerness and taste in. It's like a flood of emotions. I'm so suddenly consumed by it but unable to stop him with my two hands. Mal has always been determined. I cannot help but lean into him. Running my hands along his chest, touching his shoulders. His neck. I love all of it.

But this shouldn't exist. There are no such things as second chances after death. I know that.

I have to stop this, but I *can't.*

18 Everything but That - Mal

I feel alive again. I feel the sun and taste the wind. I don't have words for how it felt to sense Flo taking my hand, the spike of adrenaline and calm seemed to absorb straight into my skin.

I looked at her and my heart started up again.

I pulled her into my lap before I could let myself think about the motion. I somehow managed to jerk my car to the side of the highway with one hand. I didn't signal or bother with a shoulder check.

I felt like I had no time left for that.

I looked at her and I never looked back.

Flo was mine again. I don't know how I knew that, but the words had taken a hold of my head.

Flo was mine again.

"Oh, I absolutely don't deserve this," she says between fevered kisses, her soft hands holding my face as she kisses me again.

I kiss her back.

I grope her ass with one hand. She fits so perfectly into my lap, oh God dammit my dick sure likes that. "This isn't okay. I'm dead. I don't get to feel like this again. I don't get to feel him."

Him? Who the fuck is him?

"Wait, what?" I ask, she kisses me again. Her clothes are damp under my hard and hungry hands. I don't want this moment ever to end. "Mal is too good for this." She whispers against my lips, kissing my chin. I breathe her in as deeply as I can. She smells like concrete soaked with rain after a thunderstorm has swept in. Sweat dampens her skin, her dark green hair so vibrant I almost can't look away from it.

"Mal is too good for this," Flo says.

Oh, so I'm *him.* I guess that was kind of obvious.

"How can I feel this? How am I going to stop kissing him? I need to stop kissing him. I need to step back and shake my head. I need to stop fucking imaging this. There are no second chances after death." Flo speaks into my neck. Flesh on flesh. God, I love this. I spread my hands out against her back and pull her tighter in against my chest.

I'm never letting her go again.

"Obviously there are second chances Pretty Girl." I groan when she snuggles in and flips her long hair back. Fuck I missed that. I missed the look of satisfaction in her glance that flashes. It leaves me deserted.

"I don't know what I did to deserve this," I admit, "and I don't know how it's possible or how it happened. But you came back, I don't know about you, but I'm not going to waste a moment arguing it!"

How many nights had I prayed for exactly this? Fantasized about it? So many moments where I swore that I would do anything for it and now that I had it.

I can't worry in the moment that it may end. It won't. It can't.

"I thought that I'd never get to see you again. I mean I could see you, but you couldn't see me and it wasn't like this. It wasn't how I wanted it, but I did this," Flo promises.

"I fucked up. You know that I know that. Everyone in Three Hill knows that. How it is possible just to start again?" she asks and I take the opportunity to kiss her chin before pulling back.

Start again? Fuck that. Starting again would involve pretending that I didn't give a shit about the green haired gorgeous chick in my lap. I'm so over that. "I don't want to start again and I don't want to question this, not even for a second," I demand but already my thoughts are fighting against the joy and panic flooding my chest.

I grip Flo's hips, brushing my thumb against a small sliver of exposed skin. She looks at me, and I look back. Whisky coloured eyes now look black. Her lips are dry and cracked. They didn't feel like that. Her mouth felt soft, ready to be kissed senseless.

She shivers under my hands. I want to dip my head and drink her in again. I can't help it. I am a dehydrated man.

"You need to head back," Flo says, rich brown eyes suddenly black and sad. Her fingers are tracing lines onto my chest. "People will be wondering what happened. You stormed out of that class like there was a fire in your pants." She laughs nervously, quietly.

The sound is relaxed but it fades fast.

I smile because I honestly can't remember what I had planned when I left that stupid class. Was I headed back to bed?

"Yeah," I say when she dips her head. I grip her hips to lift her out of my lap but keep a hold of her hand. Our fingers intertwine as she curls into the seat. I keep looking back at her as I slip back onto the road and haul my ass out of the ditch, so terrified that she will disappear again.

I make a U-Turn and head back. Nothing about the highway makes any sense. Passing cars are meaningless as they speed away from me into the distance. I don't understand this. My mind is unable to process what the fuck just happened. I blink and blink again. What was my plan?

My body was acting as if Flo and I had made a suicide pact. Is that where I was headed? Silence and desolation?

No. I wouldn't do that. Not to my mom. Not to my dad. I won't. I can't.

Am I dead?

Is that why Flo is holding my hand? Fuck. What a strange feeling that is. I can't get used to it. I run my thumb over her white and pasty skin. She's cold and wet. Her nails are chipped.

Black nail polish.

I smile. I can't help it.

Flo was always good at that, at being different and looking damn hot doing it. She stood out. Her glance is quickly becoming heated. Fuck I miss that because I still don't have it.

I can't get it back. I know that.

Three Hill isn't as beautiful or as haunted on the way back in. All of the cars and people I pass are simply meaningless. I run my thumb along Flo's hand. She hasn't spoken, her soft and pale face is a mask. She only looks ahead, but I don't want to ask what happened.

What is it like? How has it been? I don't want to know any of that but if she wants to tell me she can. I just won't ask.

I park in the same spot I vacated, in front of a smooth looking bench, under a canopy of hanging branches.

I have to let go of her hand to kill the engine and exit. The loss of contact punches a hole into my chest. I need her skin on skin. I keep my eyes on her as I move around the hood. Flo doesn't even flinch. Her eyes remain flat when I open her door and pull on her hand.

She melts against my chest.

I'm thankful that no one else is around to see us like this. I don't know how I would explain it. Oh hey, guys look at that? My dead best friend just came back! I know that at some point now I need to ask, but first I want her in my bed. We need to get reacquainted.

"Let's get inside, your clothes are wet and normally I'd be worried about you getting sick but..." I try to laugh, but my chest seizes when she squeezes my hand back, my heart goes cold with the words she says: "I'm dead and corpses can't get sick."

"Don't say that." I keep my voice against the top of her head.

"Why not?" she asks.

"I'm not into necrophilia last time I checked, and I want to take you to bed." Again I squeeze her hand. Again she squeezes back.

I unlock my front door and lead her in. Giving her a tour of the living room and the kitchen.

She nods polity but acts like she's already seen all of it. She trails her fingers against the toaster.

She pulls away from me only for me to pull her right back in. "No way. I'm not doing that. Don't lock me out of your head. I've already been through that. If something is wrong, then say it."

"I can't," she says.

"Yes, you can." I pull her against my back by clasping her hands over my stomach, leading her up the stairs and into the darkness.

I'm nervous. I've never been nervous like this but everything about this moment feels precious. As if it could be stolen at any moment and I'm still trying to wrap my brain around it.

My girl came back.

I cross my arms over her hands as we reach the top of the stairs with loud and heavy footsteps, stumbling past the bathroom and down the hall. My bedroom door is open, just like I left it.

"Are you okay with this?" I have to ask; I feel my Pretty Girl mumble into my back. "Yeah," she says, still sounding sad.

I pull us into my bedroom, praying that she ignores the heaping mess of clothes and empty laundry baskets. I unlock our hands, turning to kick my door closed as Flo sits gingerly on the edge of my bed. Darkness settles in. I can't look anywhere but at her soft expression, my dark walls are meaningless. The posters staring back at me are blurs that are all faceless.

My bed is unmade, just how I left it.

Her hands clench around my mattress. Nails are digging in to the fabric. My white sheets are pooled around her hips, my pillows a mess. I always sleep with at least six.

The space between us flaming red with passion and words left unsaid. Moments slipping through my outstretched hands, I have her back.

"What happened?" I have to ask even though I said I wouldn't. The words escape my lips, and there's nothing that I can do to stop them. I look down when Flo laughs. Why am I so intent on ruining this?

"I panicked. That's what happened. I was alone and driving back to see you again when I panicked. I couldn't do it. I kept picking up my phone to shoot you a text, and I knew that you would text back. I just couldn't do it. I couldn't intrude on your happiness. You were doing so good, and I wasn't and I didn't know how to handle it. Everything was just going to shit. I dropped out of college. I had to figure out how to pay my loan back, and I couldn't find any work within a ten-mile radius. I was always sad and I felt broken and I didn't know how to fix it," Flo says, shaking hair around her head, trying to hide her expression.

I step forward and push the strands back.

"Did you fix it?" I don't want to sound like an ass, but this is a thought in my head that needs to be said. Flo needs to know the anger that I'm holding back.

Her regret is obvious.

"No of course I didn't fix it. What kind of question is that Mal? I was an idiot, and I made a stupid decision. I don't even know if I did it for attention or just to feel something. I don't know why I did but what sucks the most about it is that I'm not the only one who has to live with it. What about my parents? I can't undo what I did to them. I know that they're both hurting, so much so that I can't even stand to look at them. I can't go back. I can't see them. I know that I could haunt them or look in on them, but my heart can't handle that kind of depression. What you felt, I understood it because I felt it. I missed you, and I felt dead knowing that I was never going to talk to you again." she says.

"When I saw the paramedics I wanted to wave my hands but I couldn't move, and I died while I was being transported. I died surrounded by strangers who didn't give a shit. They were talking about their summer plans and their kids and asshole husbands. All I wanted to talk about was the fact that I was never going to get to live again. I witnessed them telling my family and my friends. My mom collapsed and asked if she could see me, but everyone said that she couldn't because I was such a mess. I was there with you when you got the text that something had happened." she says.

"Didn't River send it? God, you should have seen the poor kid. He felt so bad for telling you about it through text message, but I was just glad someone did. You were the first person I thought of, and I've been thinking about you ever since. I can't get you out of my head. I wanted my parents to call yours so you could come to the hospital and hold my hand. I thought that would bring me back. How stupid is that?" she asks.

I have dropped to my knees in front of her without realizing it, reaching out for her trembling hands.

"It's not stupid," I promise. "None of what you just told me is stupid, it's just honest. When I got the text message, the text message that just said 'Flo is dead,' I lost it. Of course, I lost it. I was so fucking mad. I tried calling your mom and then your dad. No one was at your house, and I tried and tried again. I just wanted to hear someone say it because that was the only way that I was ever going to believe it."

I found her dad, alone in the basement of Flo's parents' duplex. It was three days after the fact, and he just looked straight through me like a dead man holding a box of photo albums.

I couldn't bear to look at them. I still can't.

"Did you know about that?" I ask, leaving words unsaid but somehow knowing that Flo was present for the worst of it.

"I did." She simply says.

I rest my head in her lap. She leans back. We fall asleep like that.

19 Can't Go Back - Flo

I pull Mal onto his bed after he starts to drift, laying him flat on his back I curl onto his stomach. Resting my head on his hard chest, I love the sound of him breathing in. I love his heartbeat. I'm drunk with it. I love this. Fuck, how did I let this happen? How did I let myself come back here with him? I'm dead and dead girls don't get second chances even though I'm sure a lot of them wish they did.

Why me?

Why us?

Why this?

"I love you Mal, do you know that?" I whisper into his chest, tracing a pattern I created in my head. "I have loved you since we were ten." I don't know why I feel the need to say this.

I just go with it.

"You were standing at the bus stop with a bunch of other kids, when some older guy showed up and started picking on one of your friends. I think his name was Alec, you stepped right in. You stood pretty tall for a ten-year-old and you held your ground. You called the big guy a tool. He almost wet himself he was so shocked. You acted like you were going to knock his lights out. You glowed."

Great. Now I feel like a tool letting all of my mushy feels out, but what's the point in stopping now?

"I fell in love with you, and I never meant to, I just didn't seem to have any control. It just happened. I looked up one day at you and you kind of smiled and kaboom, I realized that I was in love with you. When we got older and started high school, my mind couldn't contain how I felt. We always used to make out and grope, but I thought it was just because I was there, and we were so close. I kept waiting for you to move on to somebody else." As I speak Mal moves, pulling me close.

"You didn't move on though; I mean not really. You slept with other girls, but you were always there when I needed you. Yeah, I was jealous as all hell but you didn't know how I felt. I never told you. I think you always thought that I was just screwing with you."

Again Mal moves, spreading my legs with one of his own. Oh yeah, that's a new move. I smile as we snuggle.

"I missed you more than you will ever know and I don't think I'll ever be able to explain how much I love you. Letting you go now might just be one of the worst things that I ever have to do." I look up to find soft green eyes peering down at me over a worried frown. His words are twisting with my own at the thought of either of us ever letting go. His voice is hard and cold and cruel.

"So don't let go," he almost shouts, and I take a minute before looking back down at his chest. This is not the time right now.

"Sleep Mal." I lean my head down. I kiss his neck, his arms and his stomach muscles through his clothes.

"I won't leave you. I'm apparently not allowed. This death grip you have on my arms should be illegal." I wouldn't give him up for the entire world, but I would give him up for himself. I know that this can't be real and when we are both forced to wake up it will hurt more than before. The pain is a hundred times worse than I can endure.

I had the taste of him in my memories and as vivid as it was, it was nothing compared to this. This is truly bliss. Everything about it. About him. I feel like a drug addict in search of another fix. I've never been a big drinker but right now I'm throwing back shots and dancing in a club all alone, my body whispering to the music. I understand every lyric. Every song about heartache is one I understand.

This is something grand.

How did I get by without this for so long? I wasn't even gone that long. I managed to run away for a whole month. Thirty days of pure fucking loneliness I was rancid with depression.

I was too terrified to reach out for the fear that no one wanted to hear my voice to begin with. No one wanted me around. I had accepted that. Convinced myself of it.

The problem with being truly sick is there is no cure for it. Death does not erase mental illness.

I am not reborn. I am still sick. Held down by it. My brain is unable to process reason. Mal could look me straight in the eyeballs and ask me to marry him right now, and I would still laugh out loud. I don't deal well with anything real.

That's why I chickened out. Am I a coward for taking the hard way out? I don't think so. I felt trapped. Alone. Like I had nowhere to go.

I could have gone home, stayed under the blankets for a while in my old bedroom. I moved out without telling Mal. I didn't want him to know, for fear that he would demand checking my new place out or he wouldn't care at all. That was the line we had drawn, the line we could not cross.

He could never care enough. Even when we fought, and he told me to get lost, I was angry that he didn't chase me down the block. Isn't that messed up? I wanted to get lost so that he would ride in and save me from my thoughts. I wanted to make him cry to understand that he felt the way I did. I always deep down felt like I was somewhat replaceable to Mal.

I needed him, and he showed up. That was never somehow enough.

I know that I'm not making any sense now. I'm sorry. I'll shut up now. I rest my head back down.

20 How Dare You? - Mal

I can't move. I don't want to.

Flo is on my chest. Curled into a small green ball and I feel alive now more than I ever thought possible. I feel real.

"I love you," I tell Flo. "I have always loved you. I'm in love with you, and I will always be in love with you."

Why does it hurt to say the truth? It shouldn't. This much I know.

I've told hundreds of girls that I loved them before now–okay, maybe not hundreds. Maybe ten or fifteen or so but you get where I'm going don't you? Why did that not hurt at all until now?

I feel broken glass whenever I try to move.

I move my hands to her back and slowly drag them down, touching all of the PG parts of Flo. The R rated is what I want right now. I won't take it though.

I would die if I woke up without her after having her back. My hands cup her ass.

"Why are you wearing such rough pants?" I ask. The hard material scrapes my skin.

I remember. Just like that. It all comes back. These are the clothes she was wearing in the description on the missing posters. The picture I shared on **Facestory**. I liked it and shared it again. No one commented. What do you even say to that?

"I'm sorry man?"

"My condolences?"

Prayers don't do shit. I know that.

"You okay my friend?" Flo asks my chin. She's awake. I already knew that because her breathing was uneven.

Can one even sleep in her condition?

To answer her question, no, I am not okay. I will never be okay again. "Did you expect to land?" I ask, moving my hands up and past her beautiful ass. I wrap an arm around her neck, looking down at her green head. Her roots are showing pretty bad.

Why is this the thing I notice? I'm such a jackass.

"When you jumped. Did you think that you should take a break for a moment and then you would land, and we would all simply be able to start again?"

I kiss her head because I can.

Flo squirms and makes me hard again. I pull her back in, breathing the scent of rain water in. This is where I belong and where I have always been, a human body pillow for my best friend.

My life is back again.

21 Jokes Forever - Flo

I smile. I laugh. I hide my face in Mal's chest. I don't just feel safe, I feel wanted. I feel like I've never been in danger. No one can say anything mean to me here. No one can make me insecure. I have no reason to doubt anything anymore.

I know that this feeling will probably wear off in about an hour. I don't care. "So what do you think about another shower?" I tease, muffling my voice into his t-shirt. My shirt has somehow ended up on the floor. Again. I don't care.

"I can't get the smell of dirt out of my hair. I don't know why that's the scent that has chosen to linger." I eye the fading, green split ends. The roots of my hair are dyed black. At the time I thought it worked.

Can you guess what I want to say here?

Here's a hint: (I don't care)

I snuggle closer. My fingers are pulling down at the hem of Mal's t-shirt. I'm surprised that he doesn't have chest hair. Does he shave? That's awkward. He's not a swimmer.

His pecs indent and smooth over. I memorize the soft skin with my fingers. He's pale at the moment, the natural golden tone less evident now than it was a few hours ago. He is soft all over but strong. I'm torn by the muscles in his arms. God dammit this makes me swoon all over. I have a thing for guys with strong arms. Especially when they wear well fitted t-shirts. I reach up to touch Mal's hair. It's long, and the ends are curled over. So dark brown it's almost black. It is soft and grab-able hair.

I want to kiss his jaw. His neck. I want to pull his whole world apart. Haven't we already been there?

22 Not Here - Mal

I kiss her, tasting her and pulling her entire world apart. I was asleep a moment ago, but now I'm here.

My hands find her hair. I use my knee to push her legs apart, actively searching for her warmth.

I need to feel every inch of her.

"Come here," I tell her.

She whispers.

"I am here."

I kiss her harder. Her lips taste sour. Her kisses are brand new and yet so familiar it hurts. I've kissed her before, of course; my body melds beneath hers. She feels sturdy in my arms and yet I'm terrified to break her apart. Her heart beats, and I'm afraid that the glass within her is about to shatter. I kiss her words apart.

23 Forever - Flo

I feel tethered and torn apart. Bruised and injured. I turn so that our chests are pressed together. I'm only in my white bra. It has been turned grey with blood and dirt. Brain matter.

I left this boy with a broken heart.

I died and yet I didn't go anywhere.

I still haven't gone anywhere.

I haven't done anything that matters.

I'm kissing my best friend, and I feel alive right down to the tips of my fingers. I open my mouth and feel devoured.

I want to devour Mal forever. I feel his hands leaving my hair, moving down my back to the clasp of my bra. He unhooks it without a care, and I try to pull back to let the fabric slide down my arms, but Mal won't let me go anywhere. The straps slip and suddenly I am still covered and yet I've never felt so open before.

I grind my hips against him when he asks for more.

I'm close, and I still want closer.

I've never felt like this before. I kiss him once more because I'm terrified of this moment being over.

I want to stay with this boy that I adore. I want to stay forever. I want more. I don't want to talk anymore.

I'm not here. I'm nowhere. My life is over. I'm doomed.

Dead from the start. There are no chances to start over.

I want a do-over.

I want-

24 Before and After - Mal

I felt her. I felt every inch of her, and I want to roll us both over. I want her beneath me. Green hair is spilling out everywhere. I want in her God damned underwear. I want her forever. I shiver and feel as if my body has been forced into a cold shower.

I open my eyes, and I'm alone in here. Flo isn't with me anymore.

I'm naked. My hands are resting against the shower. What am I doing in here? Where am I? Why is my face covered in tears?

How did I get here?

"This isn't funny." I cry out, spitting blood out of my mouth. I feel like I got punched in the throat. It hurts to blink, to talk. I might choke if I try to shout. I can't stand still.

I need to lie down.

I am alone.

"Hello?" no one responds to me, no one at all. Like I always said and thought a hundred fucking times or so: I am completely alone.

I don't have Flo.

Fuck.

I need to lie down.

25 No! - Flo

No! No! No! I have been turned backwards and inside out. I fly into the wall of Mal's dark bedroom and feel my heart give out.

I'm dead. I'm cold.

No!

My ass lands against the hard ground. I have reached out and pulled a handful of posters down. I look at the crumbles mess of cartoons; super hero and super villain's. None of these means anything to the man that I'm in love with. He collected them when he was a kid because of his dad. His dad loved comics.

Mal loved singing. Dancing. Math. Mal was a weird kid. That's why I loved him. That's why I still love him and scream until my voice threatens to shatter my head. I need to stand but instead I slam my body back. I felt him. I was back, for like half of a hot second, but I was still back. I felt it. I had it.

Just like that.

I felt my body being pulled apart like a rubber band. It hurts, and my jaw feels slack. I think I busted my hip. My tooth stabbed through my lip. I'm a mess.

Mal groans and rolls over, rubbing at his face as if I wasn't just with him, on top of him, topless, and under him, kissing his neck.

He's in pain. I can hear it.

What the hell happened? I try to stand. Something loud has stabbed into the palm of my hand. I try to focus on it but the frame starts to fade to black, and I know that this is almost it, but I'm not about to let myself burn out like that again. I don't want to fade to black.

I want to be epic and ever-present. I want a second chance. I see it, and I know that I have to grasp it. Just a random image, like a **PicChat**. I know that it's about to be deleted, but I hold my thumb down to save it. I see a lifetime flash. The possibilities. A chance. I have to take it.

The universe doesn't have to ask.

I stand and watch the world as I know it fade to black.

26 The First Kiss of Death - Cadence

I woke up on my back in my kitchen. I was staring up at blank ceiling that stared right back. My heart was a hammer in my chest, and I had no idea what the fuck had happened.

I still don't know what happened.

I haven't found the strength to get up just yet. I was facedown into my vomit, yeah that was fantastic. I rolled over and wiped my mouth off, ridding my face of most of it.

My mouth tastes fantastic. Like ass. Old food and teeth that haven't been brushed since...God I can't even remember when. I have become that much of a mess that collapsing in my vomit wasn't the surprise that it should have been, but waking up like this is.

I heard a voice I didn't recognize, a scream that didn't make any sense and a strange pressure in my chest.

I felt like I had invited some ugliness in.

Yeah, that makes no sense. I blink and blink again. I feel like death. I almost always feel like this the day after well, *that.* That's what I want to call it, just *that.* Not my drunk sluttiness. Not a night out on the town that always ended up with me on my back on a mattress. Not me regretting my choices. Just *that.* It happens again and again and I am not powerless to stop it: that thing that happened and cannot be taken back.

I just don't know anything different. Hello, my name is Cadence Smalls. I'm twenty-seven. Five-foot-five-and-a-half, my hair is dyed a terrible red and my gel nails desperately need to be filled in.

I am an addict.

I am desperate. I am a fuck up. I am hardly ever missed.

I move my hands to the floor to push myself off of my back; I turn, and my hair falls on my face. I blow on it, trying to brush it back with the back of my vomit-smeared hand. I'm not wearing much, a slinky black dress and some sandals that are only hanging on now by the thin silver straps. My ankles are in a death trap. I try to slide them off with my hands but fail quite epically at that.

My kitchen is a mess. The floor stained with remnants of last night party fest. You know, just the usual events of me and a bottle of vodka cuddled against my chest.

My roommate is MIA again. Not that I should be at all surprised by that fact, Torrance doesn't like to come home if he can help it. Not that I blame him. I wouldn't come home either if I had a different option, but I don't. This apartment is my prison. The pale green walls I painted with my best friend during a night high on energy drinks and sedatives. The door has ten deadbolts in it. The fridge is filled with alcohol.

I make myself stand and almost stumble backwards. Reaching out to the kitchen table, I slap the wood with my hand. It stings for about half a second. I live in a small two-bedroom basement apartment just off of campus. I have lived here for a year and a half with Torrance.

He is my younger brother's best friend. He's a good kid. I am an awful influence for him. He knows it. I avoid it.

My hair usually reaches my shoulders when it isn't in such a mess. I desperately need to wash it and brush it. Possibly untangle it, spray it down with some super disinfectant. I am totally the definition of a hot mess, Only without the "hot" part.

The bathroom is located right off of the kitchen. My bedroom is next but the door is closed, and I don't want to risk opening it.

I don't know if I have any more guests. I don't want to risk running into any of them.

I need to strip and shower, wash myself of any and all sins. I need to rinse off the evidence and shave my armpits. They are starting to inch.

As is my lady business.

That's right. I said it. Deal with it.

I turn on the bathroom light and glower at the disgusting damp towel and piss puddle mess that has now soaked into the small shower mat. It used to be purple; at least it was when I was regularly washing it. The laundry room and I are no longer friends. I look into the mirror, and the death of my best friend looks back.

I didn't ask for this.

No one asks for life to end, but the world is a cruel place and change only happens when you least expect it. My usually happy brown eyes look black, and my face is a blotchy, red mess.

It has been like this since the moment that I found out my little brother, my best friend, wasn't coming back.

Every day I think about Alex. It has been like this all of the two-thousand-five-hundred-and-fifty-five days since it happened. He is every pain in my chest and everything about my old life that I miss.

He was my best friend. My only sibling. My other half. My better half. I was supposed to protect him, and take care of him and keep him sheltered from all of the bad. Instead I pushed him into it and failed at being a big sister, I failed at being the person he needed me to be, and now he's dead. I did this.

Everything that happened? Well, I'm to blame for it.

I can't stand my own reflection.

I pick up my toothbrush and soak it under the tap before covering it in my favourite minty goodness. I stick my toothbrush into my mouth and give my teeth and gums a good bath. Rinse. Spit. Rinse. Spit. I do this like ten times just because I know that I need it.

I close the door with my foot and peel off what's left of my tiny black dress. I'm not wearing a bra, or underpants. I have no class. I'm spastic. I turn on the shower and push back the curtain. Someone had sex in here last night; I can still smell it.

How nasty is that?

I don't even know if I was a participant.

I step in and almost slip because I don't have a shower mat. I used to; at least I think that I did. Torrance must have gotten rid of it.

Stupid kid.

The water hits me with a vengeance. I deserve every burn mark from it. The temperature scalds and I welcome it. I let it. I could kill it. But that would be bad.

It's while I'm standing naked, letting the worst of myself in that I see it: a memory. A flash, neon green and vibrant. I see a casket.

It's all gone before I can remember where the hell I saw it. Probably on Webflix. My laptop has become my only friend, my blood relative.

It's always there when I need it. The relaxing hum of my favourite movie playing again. This week it's a romantic novel, film adaptation. Next week it might be something so bad and cheesy, I can't even watch it.

I'm freaky like that.

I wash my hair about ten times; I just want to make it soft again. My constant dye jobs have almost killed it. I have wicked split ends.

I turn off the water even though there are still bubbles on my skin. I reach for a towel and pull it on, wrapping the towel around my boobs, the soft fabric hanging right below my ass.

I forgot to shave my armpits.

Fuck.

I grab a pair of pants off of the magazine rack we keep in the bathroom, loaded down with reading material for my many male guests. Not all of which are mine. Some belong to Torrance.

I pull my pants on under my towel. I do not even believe that they are my own. I think they belong to some random dude.

I swap out my towel for a shirt that I found in the hall. It's light blue and super comfortable, sewn together out of clingy material. I drop my still soaked towel onto the ground. I know that I need to check out my bedroom. The scene of the crime if you will.

One night stands are my thing now. It's the only time that I don't feel. The only way for me to let my mind go, blocking everything about me out. I don't remember last night's dude very well. I think he was cute, at least somewhat decent down south.

You know, dick wise and all.

I knock on the door just to be polite before turning the knob and stepping forward with both eyes closed.

I'm such a chicken shit I tell yeah.

"Come out, come out wherever you are!" I call, opening my eyes one at a time, and only after peeking through my fingers.

My room is empty, but the bed is a disaster zone if I've ever seen one. There are pink sheets and fluffy white pillows all over the ground. I check the garbage just to make sure that the condom got thrown out. I cover it with a tissue.

As if any of this will help.

I know that it won't.

27 I'm Fucked up, and I Know It - Mal

I don't know what happened. I remember being at school and coming back. I remembering being at the park, again and again, staring at a grave that just stares right back.

I'm in my bed again. I left the shower running and climbed into my sheets naked. My birthday suit is soaked in sweat. I'm sick, a demon that can't be fixed. I imagined that she came back to life again.

How pathetic is that?

How twisted and sick?

I feel like a God damn idiot.

I breathe in.

I hear a knocking downstairs. Soft but persistent. I roll onto my back and reach for my phone. I think I left it on the table beside my bed, but I can't find it. The sound knocks again.

My head aches. My chest is throbbing. I want to puke and piss. I feel sick. I reach over the edge of my mattress to pick up a pair of sweats. I don't know what I find, but I think it's blood red. I swing my legs around push my legs into the holes and pull the fabric up and over my dick. Tying the rope into a bow that looks more like a drunk ribbon.

I force myself to stand.

My bedroom is pitch black. I have no idea what time it is, but I push my curtains back. The weather outside is sunshiny and golden.

Fuck that shit. I let my curtains fall back.

My bedroom is a mess. It always has been. The hardwood floor is covered in clothes and blankets and damp towels.

I am a mess.

The floor creaks with my every tired step. I push my hair back; I don't bother stopping to look at myself in the hallway mirror because I have no use for the person who looks back.

The man I was is dead.

The man I am doesn't have a name yet.

The small hallway upstairs ends at the staircase that leads into the main floor. My townhouse isn't massive, but it's decent. I was lucky and privileged enough to snag the end unit. Meaning I only have neighbours on the one side, they don't make noise.

I make enough of it.

The noise knocks and knocks again. The strange noise has a soft edge to it; gentleness edged with perseverance.

I'm annoyed. I can't help it. People have been stopping in since well, you know when. Since it all happened, since the papers got word of it, and her face ended up splashed on every local news station. They even had a helicopter filming live footage fly over the cliff, zooming in on her body.

Once the search team discovered it, an anonymous call came in...

A jumper.

A girl.

Ruthie Jane.

Flo.

My heartbeat had jumped; I wasn't around to catch it.

In that moment my life had started to end but I'm still alive, I still somehow exist and I don't understand it. I hit the steps one heavy foot a time with a heavy and memory filled head.

I am dead.

"I'm coming, shut up," I warn, calling out to the door in the kitchen. I have two doors: one in the living room, and one in the kitchen. Both lead outside. Both have locks and windows next to them.

My townhouse has an awesome set up to it. My kitchen is grotesque. The fridge full of rotting food. Expired milk. The table is covered in bills and garbage. The floor is sticky with spilled shit.

Like gin.

I like gin.

I unlock the door and pull it open. My eyes are taking the girl before me in. She comes up to like my chin; her eyes are dark and stained red. Her skin, pale and blotched, is a complete mess.

She's holding a tray of something I automatically fear might be poisonous. "What's this?" I ask, kicking myself and biting my lip. That sentence is not how I wanted to start this. This, whatever this is.

"It's a sandwich," the girl says, "a ham sandwich and some cheese crackers, and some chocolate with a side of friendship."

Her words seem heavy, filled with a silent expectation.

I try to take her strange expression in. Her hair is dyed what I think must be an attempt at pumpkin orange, with brown roots sticking out the top of a hairstyle that was started, but never finished. It hangs past her face in ringlets. Soft brown eyes take me in. So much like Flo's that I suddenly feel sick. I hate the resemblance, no matter how fleeting it is.

"I heard you could use a friend," the girl says, and I'm so stunned by the audacity and strangeness of what she said, that I don't even try to block her when she invites herself in.

"Not really but I could use the sandwich." I watch her make herself at home in my kitchen. My eyes are dropping to her round hips.

Round ass.

Even in grey sweatpants and a red top made of nothing but the slinkiest of fabric, this strange girl makes me breathless. I don't like that. I also don't like the fact that I can't take my eyes off of her curved back. Short legs and large breasts just begging for my attention. She's all torso from what my eyes can grasp.

I want her out of my kitchen.

"Do you always stare at everyone like that?" the intruder asks, unwrapping the tray and setting it down. Her hands are careful with the heavy glass. She's delicate. I don't get it.

"Get out of my kitchen!" I demand. "I'm not doing this. Whoever you are and whatever you want, you're not going to get it. I'm in no mood to be used for information about the death of my best friend. I get that this town is small, and this story is massive but get the fuck over it. I sure as hell am." This is complete and utter bullshit, but I don't give a shit. The story about Flo is only massive because there is nothing else in Three Hill quite like it.

Our crime rate is non-existent. When we have a problem, we bury it.

"I'm Cadence." The girl laughs, not at all threatened by my childish temper. "And I don't want anything, I don't know about your friend and I don't want to talk about it. I just want to be your friend," her words seem genuine, but yeah, I've heard about a thousand versions of what she just said. Every one of those conversations haunts the back of my head.

"Get out. Leave the sandwich but take the chocolate."

"Yes sir."

Cadence mocks me with a smile that makes my stomach swell with nervousness.

I hate this feeling. I hate it. I want to murder it. I never want to feel that way again. I promised.

"Get out." I say again. I can't stop saying it. I can't explain the anger that flares out into my expression, but whatever Cadence sees in it, she seems to understand. She's not afraid of me.

"Okay. I can do that, but I'm not taking the chocolate. Only because if I take it home with me I can't promise that I won't eat it."

"Fantastic." I bullshit.

She makes everything nice and pretty on the counter before turning back towards me, bumping my chest with her shoulder. I don't think that this move is by accident. I feel nothing awkward in the contact. I just feel flesh.

Her glance is finally gracing mine with its presence. She is about to leave and that should be that but for some reason it isn't.

"It's not your fault," Cadence says without one hint of rudeness or cruelness. Brown eyes shine, reaching somewhere deep down inside of me and twisting my heart in her fist. "You should know that."

I close the door behind her with a slam.

28 Who Is That? - Cadence

I sit in the living room after brushing my hair and getting dressed, staring off into the dead air that is my television set.

I haven't paid the cable bill yet.

What time is it?

I glance over my shoulder to look for Torrance, which is stupid since I would have heard him come in. Poor kid. He looks a lot like Alex, except for the dark blond hair and the blue eyes. His innocence though, my brother was all about that. The resemblance is fading but I long to see it, I think the only reason I originally moved in with him was to protect him, to take care of him.

I can't do that, and he is a grown man, almost the same age that Alex would have been. I feel like an ancient old troll compared to him even though when I look in the mirror, I know that I don't look twenty-seven.

I just look lifeless.

Tiny framed and a giant, but still somehow curvaceous.

I need to get out of this place. I should go look for Torrance. See what kind of trouble he's gotten himself in.

Yeah.

That's not going to happen. I have the sudden urge to get off of my ass and make a sandwich: a ham sandwich. I also want chocolate. I must be getting my period. Thank God for that. It's better than being knocked up by a man now rendered nameless. I try not to remember any of my one night stands.

I get up. One step. Two step. I can do this. I can eat. Nothing truly bad can come of that. Can it?

I walk back into the kitchen. The floor is still a mess of vomit, and something weird inside of me is pushing me to clean it. Wash away the demons.

Yeah. I want to scream, *as if.* But I do it. Somehow and for some reason, I dip into the hallway closet to retrieve the mop bucket. The mop itself is grey and gross looking as shit. The strands are completely solid. I don't have anything to swap it with. So I pick up the bucket and mop, carrying it into the kitchen.

I set it on the counter top and turn on the tap. The sink is filled with gross dirty dishes. I hate touching shit like that. I reach into the drawer where the forks and knifes live and pull out a pair of pink rubber gloves I forgot that I had. They have rhinestones. Glitter all along the fingertips. They must belong to Torrance. He's a closeted drama queen like that.

I pull them on and reach for the dish soap or whatever is left. I need to go to the store and get on top of all of this shit. I grab a wash cloth and get at it. Washing one dish. A cup. A coffee mug.

This is disgusting, and I hate it. I am so afraid of bugs. Eww! Something slimy touched me! Get it off! Get it off!

I fling something that does not look edible and or human onto the back of the sink. There's a window right above it, a window that I blocked off with newspapers and a magazine print off. I can't even remember what it looks out on. Sunshine? A garden? The street?

I've been holed up in my dread for so long I don't even think it's possible anymore to pull my head out of my ass. I'm locked up by a fucked up thought process. But this is my punishment, and I deserve it.

I deserve seclusion.

I don't deserve to live.

29 What the Actual Frack? - Cadence

I bought an old car that barely runs. I don't remember when but I know that it happened. I took out the money for it because buying it meant helping some poor old woman. I guess the old beater belonged to one of her kids, or her kid. I can't remember how many she had.

It belonged to a girl. She didn't say much more than that. I only knew about the woman and her kid because of Torrance. He knew them. He wanted to buy the car but couldn't afford it, so I bought it for him and said he could pay me back. He still hasn't used it.

It barely runs, but it gets me to work and back. I have to work to pay the rent. I hate this, but it is just the way life is.

I start the car with the remote before getting in. It's warm out today and for the first time in months I convince myself that I can almost feel it. I want to close my eyes and take it in. The problem with this is that by letting the warmth in, I allow myself to feel all too much of it. Once I turn my heart on it's hard to shut it down again.

I would rather be a robot. Turning everything off meant that I could somehow get through it. I could feign normal actions before returning to the darkness. This is how I get through it. I fake it.

I don't know where I'm headed. I think I traded shifts today with some short, pimply faced red-headed kid. I work as a cashier at a gas station. It doesn't pay much but no one talks to me, and that's enough. My mind revels in the silence. I find comfort in it.

I take a left out of the parking lot and straight into busier traffic.

Three Hill only has three intersections. I find the first one and avoid it, carefully watching the road ahead.

I changed after washing the dishes, even though there wasn't a point in it. I pulled on one of my worst shirts.

The kind fused together with clingy fabric that hangs and hugs every indecent curve. Every flab of fat. Every roll that I have on my back. I wipe my sweaty palms off on my pants.

I eat to make myself feel better, I know that. I've gotten quite good at it; I want to stop at the drive-thru for McDonald's and I plan on it. But that doesn't explain why I'm holding a cake pan on my lap. I made two sandwiches and stuffed in some chocolate. The cheese and crackers were a last ditch totally random plan.

I still have no idea where I'm headed. All I know is that I need to get there fast. I can't explain it. The second row of thought's currently present in my head, a strange new awareness.

Like the queen Beyoncé said:

I woke up like this.

30 Bring the World Back - Cadence

I saw him. You know, the dude with black hair and green eyes more beautiful than the most luscious of forests.

He was way taller than I am, with naturally tanned olive skin. A strong jawline and lips bruised and picked at. A fresh layer of scruff and redness coating his skin. He slammed his door in my face right after I intruded on him.

Seriously. He opened the door, and I walked right in. Who does that?

I wish I could explain the way I knew what to say to him, how to find him. He is a stranger. That was the first time that I had ever seen him, but somehow I know that it won't be the last.

My body flooded with relief the instant that our eyes met, and I know that that doesn't make any fucking sense.

I don't know him.

I would have no reason to know him or to want to know him. Seeking him out to run into him would be pointless. As far as I know we don't have any friends in common, and yet here I am, sitting in my Old beater. I've been staring at his front door since he slammed it. He lives in a student housing complex. The nicer side of it. The front yard is fenced in. He seriously has a white picket fence.

There are trees. Beautiful and strong. Dense.

He is hidden behind his small forest. I left the food with him and for some reason I sincerely hope that he eats it. He didn't look well. His strong jaw was hanging open.

He was shirtless, completely and almost one-hundred-percent naked. My eyes scanned his hard chest. His arms, broad shoulders. They were taut with impatience. I looked down out of habit and saw what looked like a six pack. He glared at me until my exit.

He forced it.

Now I'm just sitting in the **Old beater** like an escaped mental patient. I need to get on with it.

Suck it up princess.

I start my engine and reverse out of the parking spot, I was parked crooked so I took up two spots. For some reason, I was in that much of a rush. I'm acting like a total nut. I need to shake this off. I tie my hair back in a bun, driving one handed until I'm done.

I swerve a little but right myself.

I decide to head to **Walmands**, the local grocery emporium. The owner is like a billionaire now or some shit, he moved down south to the U.S. Our **Walmands** is just one out of thousands, but it's also one of the biggest. I applied there a few months back but when I came in wasted they told me that the position I wanted was no longer open.

Of course it wasn't. I drive around the back, behind the hardwood store located right next to it. My dad warned me against doing this. Mostly because driving over nails and shit is bad.

I still do it.

I park behind a white van. The kind that kidnappers purchase. Bad men with 1970's pornstaches.

I didn't bring my purse in, just my wallet. I tuck it into my armpit.

I get out, locking my car walking quickly, head down, orange hair flying back. I'm a train wreck, and I know it. At least when faced with a train wreck, most decent people avoid it. Other assholes stare at it.

The parking lot is massive but I parked near the handicap section, next to a tree and a bush. There's a whole twenty-some steps between me and the front entrance. I run them.

The automatic doors swish open. I enter in the exit.

"Hey guys, look who is it?" the whispers come from behind my back, as soon as I walk in.

I nod at an old woman wearing a blue vest: the welcome wagon. She's guarding the shopping carts and the flyer/coupon bin. I walk with hesitance.

"Isn't that Cadence? Man, I haven't seen her since..."

Since when? Last weekend, when I got wasted enough to forget the run in?

"...since they told us Alex wasn't going to make it."

Seven years and counting.

"She looks like crap, Jesus."

I already know that. I didn't need a kid who looks younger than Torrance to tell me that. They've gathered right next to a discount candy rack. Three of them, the ass-hat and two girls who eye me over paper cups probably filled with some diet soda.

I don't look at them. I don't need to hear them say my little brothers name for it all to be brought back; I already have that. I just walk, eyes ahead, heart dead. I've gotten good at it.

31 But It Is - Mal

I eat fast and crawl back into bed with my chocolate. It's delicious. Creamy and milky and perfect.

The woman in me loves it. The man that I am just feels feminine. I have a television set up on my dresser, and I'm currently holding the remote for it. I start flipping past boring news programs.

The world has gone to complete shit, but I am totally, one-hundred and-twenty-five-percent aware of that. I don't need graphic images to remind me of it. The destruction is fact. It's impossible to escape it.

I click the red END button and close my eyes against the sudden silence. I need a drink. I need a fresh air. I need to have a shit. I need to shower again.

I gave up looking for my phone because a part of me doesn't care to find it. I'm terrified to hear her voice again, and yet I'm terrified to erase them; voicemails, pictures, video attachments.

I can't handle it. Not yet.

I start wondering if I smashed it into pieces, I almost remember doing that, why would I do that?

I cling to every memory of Flo with self destruction. The idea that I may have cost myself all that I had left of her voice, photographs of her stupid lips, is like cutting open my own flesh.

I roll onto my stomach, kicking at my blankets and holding onto my pillow as my eyes burn. I refuse to cry again.

Grief is weakness. Acceptance is moronic.

I slip off my pants and strut back downstairs towards the kitchen. I grab some milk out of the fridge and sniff test it. Everything I have to drink is rancid.

I vomit.

I don't bother cleaning it. I just try not to step in it.

32 I Will Not Ask for Help - Mal

I think that its Friday now. It must be. My heart swells at the thought of the weekend's fast approach. Two more days alone. Two days where I don't have to feel bad about not going to school. Not that I ever really feel bad at all but it's not like I have anything better to do. Fucking wonderful.

I woke up alone. I know that this is my normal now. I showered and wolfed some cereal down. I went to the store last night to buy milk. I only left the house because I needed to. I drove the whole way with all four windows rolled down and the radio on loud.

No one bothered me. It was cool. I have decided today to go to school. Because trying again won't kill you, right?

If only one could murder an already bruised and battered soul and I don't think it's truly possible. I'm dead anyhow.

I get dressed in my douche bag clothes: Ed Hardy shirt, my blue jeans with the pockets bejewelled. I feel like a total tool, and I look like one too. Ha, cool.

I head outside and start my Chevy™. Once again, I could walk to school but I'm still a lazy asshole. I have only just hopped in when I feel a strange chill, I look over and see the wacko girl from a few days ago. Cadence, or something like that? Who the hell knows?

I don't care to be quite honest with you.

"Can I help you?" I call out, rolling my window down. She's sitting on a rock placed in front of the parking lot. I think the rock has some dedication etched into it. She doesn't look confused, her brown eyes purposeful.

"Nope, not at all." Wacko girl smiles. Lifting up her coffee as if to toast me a farewell. "Just checking up on you."

Okay, that's not strange at all.

I nod and turn the wheel.

I have almost no good memories of this hellhole. This is my second year, and I still haven't accomplished shit all. I'm in open studies, and the government was so happy to help me add to my collective debt pile that they gifted me with another four-thousand-dollar student loan. It was deposited into my account on the first actual day of classes.

I blew half of it on my rent, the rest went to random crap. Car insurance. A new paint job. Some fancy ass pants.

I'm a moron like that.

I park my ride sideways against a minivan and hop out. Closing my door with a slam but making sure to lock it. I didn't bring any books or notepads, or my backpack. I don't need shit.

The entire school is made of brick. The front entrance made of half a dozen metal doors, all painted blood red. People are everywhere. Normal humans. Functioning people without heads full of useless brain mucus. I nod at someone I don't know one the way in. I think it was one of River's friends. You know, the douche bag that she always wanted. She being my bestest and deadest friend. Scratch that, you didn't need to know that. I duck my head. The front entrance isn't silent, but noise doesn't jump out at me the way that I expected.

This seems okay. I think I can handle this.

33 Second Chances Suck Ass - Mal

I don't know what my first scheduled class is. I just kind of kick a door open and strut through it. I turn a few heads on my way in, blondes, brunettes and redheads. All chicks. All hot. Is this some sort of feminist power rant class? That would be excellent.

I grin.

I sit in an empty seat. Near the back. An aisle seat so everyone has to climb over me to get in. Rows and rows of auditorium style chairs with desks that barely double as an arm rest. Everyone in the same row has no choice but to get acquainted fast. When a cute blonde slips past me I take the chance to brush my hand against her firm ass. The blush of her cheeks has me squirming in my seat.

Other people start piling in, and I watch the old dude down at the front of the class, the bottom of the mosh pit. The professor. He's dressed in a sweat vest and dark denim pants. He has an iPad in his hand and turns to pull down the projection screen, with boredom.

Why does he deserve my attention? The answer to my question, of course is quite obvious: He doesn't.

34 You Did Exactly That - Mal

I enjoy my first class, even though I don't understand any of it. I spent the rest of my morning as a shut in, waiting for the afternoon and for the incoming thunderstorm to kick in.

When it rained, I felt her again.

That's how it had always been, even before her death. Ruth was and is the only person in my life who had ever made a difference. I use her birth name now because that's what her headstone says.

Ruthie Jane.

Loving friend.

Daughter,

I will forever wait for us to be together.

I hate those words. I don't know who chose them or who put them there but there they are. Forever. I stay inside until the storm starts, and then I head out to my car. I should have worn my jacket, something warmer than a t-shirt.

I get into my car but roll the windows down just so that I can still feel the weather. I turn on the radio. I want something soft to linger and maybe draw us together? As if I can get lost in the world if I only try harder. I miss her. I need her. I can't do this without her.

I start to drive and even thinking hurts. Breathing in glass shards of memories that have been torn apart and shattered.

Is this what it feels like? Being forced to start over? How does this work? Is it supposed to hurt? Would it be easier if I just tried to forget her? Does that make me a jerk? Honestly, right now I would be up for anything that didn't hurt. I guess I just always thought that we would end up together you know? Even if she wasted her time dating some random fucktard, I would be able to get through the next ten years, as long as I knew that someday we would end up together.

That was how this was supposed to work. Instead, she's dead and not having her hurts to much for words.

I don't want to start over.

I decide to head to the grocery store. Mostly because I'm out of beer, and I know that they sell it there. I don't even like beer. To me, it tastes bitter. I drink it because I'm bored, something to get me numb and tide me over for the next few hours.

I get drunk because I'm bored. It's the only time I ever feel alright anymore. Even if everything I do while hammered ends up being things that I can't remember.

Making mistakes is hard. It's even harder when you're sober.

35 Kiss Me and Think of Her, You Turd - Cadence

I have momentarily forgotten how to get home from here, not the grocery store. It feels like it's been a few days since I've been there. I know that in reality, it has probably only been a few hours. I'm at a plus sized bitches store.

Why? I can't remember. I'm wearing the same clothes that I remember pulling on before, I lift a hand and realize that my hair is still everywhere. I'm standing in the back of a store.

I glance into a mirror and hate what I see there. I look tired. My brain hurts. I keep trying to remember how I got here but so far, none of my usual reminders work.

I have my car. Good car. I'm wearing my bracelets. My elastic band reminder than I snap whenever my heart hurts. The stinging on my wrist is a good distraction. It almost always works. Not today.

All I can hear is the rainstorm pounding against the windows and the roof, it's peaceful. I want to go outside and stand between the parked cars. Letting my clothes become soaked and tattered. I want to feel. I want to feel like I matter, like I'm really here. I haven't felt like in forever.

There was one moment, one small almost meaningless moment when I woke up on my kitchen floor, when my lungs didn't hurt anymore. One moment when my body wasn't sore, when it didn't feel like I had murdered my liver. I blinked and no sooner had the moment disappeared. I felt empty after, left with only a strange anger that lingered, drawing me towards a stranger, his lean body offered comfort even from a distance.

As soon as Mal was near I felt better.

I couldn't touch him of course, or utter a truthful word and this made me feel worse. I look around the store. There's a lady at the cash register. She's dressed in comfortable formal wear: a purple turtle neck sweater, her light hair cut in a fashionable peacock style–kind of like all those women on TLC. The one with eight kids and a nasty divorce? Yeah, she's got crazy-eight hair.

The cashier fearfully looks me over. I realize how strange I look standing here, trembling fingers. I secretly want to burst into tears, but I also don't want to be forcefully kicked out of here.

I grab a sweater off of the hanger.

"Can I try this on please?" I ask a little too loudly, the woman cringes, ducking her ears between her shoulders before eyeing the counter. She picks up a key and starts towards me, manoeuvring herself around displays and security features. The change rooms are in the back of the store. I keep my head down, waiting to follow her. I'm nervous.

More self-conscious than ever before, I want to have another shower. I want to stand outside and cry to be run over.

"You'll have to leave your purse at the cash counter." The sales woman nods, quiet but assertive with her assumption of me.

"I don't have my bag, I don't think," I say, looking around me with what feels like a heavy worry on my face. I feel the fake pockets on my pants for my wallet but the fabric lays flat.

The cashier doesn't step back.

I can hear the thoughts screaming from inside of her head: *poor girl, she has no way to pay for that. I wonder what happened. I can tell that she hasn't had a bath. Maybe she's homeless.* I just want to put the stupid sweater back.

"I'm sorry I bothered you, I think I forgot my purse at home or in my car I don't know." I put the sweater down on the ground, kneeling to keep her from seeing my tears that have started spilling down.

How did I end up here? How did I drive here completely zoned out? For the first time in a long while, I'm actually afraid of myself.

36 Fall for You - Mal

I'm watching her. The orange-haired girl. I caught a random glimpse of her through a store window. I pulled over.

I had to.

Even as I pulled over I knew that I would eventually have to get out. It felt wrong staring at her while I sat in my Chevy™. I felt like someone on a stake out, only without any true motive at all. I had no urge to figure this girl out; getting close to someone new wasn't what I needed right now. It wasn't something that I could handle. I watched her anyhow, with all four of my windows rolled down, my arms getting totally soaked.

I folded myself out onto the road and stood, tall and hallow. I moved around to lean against the passenger side door and cross my arms against the rain, even though I'm not cold.

I can't fight a chill I don't feel.

I took a shortcut home, through downtown.

This is not the way that I normally go. There are a dozen little shops, lining each side of the small and narrow road. All in a row. I don't even know the name of the one that she's in right now. The orange-haired girl.

Cadence. I take a look around, the store is small and it seems to cater to luscious women such as her. I watch her curves as she moves, her bottom lifted up by the clingy material of her denim leggings. Guilt wedges its way into my heart, I shouldn't be checking this girl out.

I can feel Flo tugging at my soul.

I squint my eyes and feel like I'm trying to figure something out, like a puzzle I can't see. I try to remember something nagging at me so loud that I want to puke, but all I get is black storm clouds. They rain down smoke.

I know what I need to do now. I push myself off of my Chevy™, and take one step, twos step and soon four.

I open the door to the clothing store and a little bell rings when I do so, alerting Cadence to my arrival.

There's a woman shopping for a new fur coat, she offers me a lip stick stained smile. I don't do anything at all. I don't nod. I don't frown. I'm a stoic asshole.

I have Cadence in my sights now. It scares me how I find her beautiful. How her eyes appear such a warm brown, even when she looks panicked and is quickly glancing around.

I like that she's tall. Well, taller than most of the girls I know. She's taller than Flo. I don't know why this fact punches me in the balls. I hate all the reminders of what I used to know but I go searching for them in haunted shadows.

I like that when she stands up and seems to forget herself, she sticks her chest out. I notice how the tops of her breasts swell out of her clothes, begging to be cuddled.

I do that well.

I like that she bites her bottom lip before she smiles. I like that she doesn't notice me at all.

I notice her frown, though.

"Who are you?" the words have left me and there is nothing that I can do. I stop, a step behind her, too far away and far too close, I stand as strong and wide as I am able. Cadence turns around, nice and slow. I swear that in this suddenly vacant room, our voices echo.

My heart is in my throat. It jumps when she says, "I don't know."

37 Fuck It - Cadence

I should shut up. Seriously. I should slam my jaw and shut it, but the stunned look on his face is totally worth what I just said.

"I don't know who I am at this exact moment. I don't even know where I am, and I realize that you probably think I'm psychotic, but I'm not going to apologize for that."

"Okay," he says.

We take a pause at that. I'm playing with my hands because I can't understand the way that I sweat while looking at this boy. This boy who is more of a man. I love the fact that his chin even has a bit of stubble on it.

I almost felt like a full on pedophile for a second. He's younger than me, I know that.

"How old are you?" I ask, because I desperately need to know this. Not that it matters, we are nothingness. I'm a stranger to him. Nothing more, nothing less.

"Twenty-one," he says, "and my name is Malachi, in case you didn't already know that, but everyone calls me Mal, so you best get used to it. I also answer to ass-hat, but I don't know why you would ever call me that."

"I wouldn't." I feel like I have. "You can call me Cadence, or Caddie Doll. Everyone calls me that." Everyone always has. Everyone but Alex. He called me Cade just because he liked it. Little brat.

I almost feel myself smile but quickly try to hide it. For some reason, I know that Mal has noticed. I can almost feel it. Yeah, that doesn't make any sense. His lips turn up the end but in an instant his face is once again, stoic. Green eyes are hiding a mountain of sadness.

I want to know this man. I want to know what makes him angry. I want to know what makes him so sad. I want to eradicate any pain that he has ever had. I've never felt like that.

38 Just Try It - Mal

I don't know how I got her outside, but I did it. Perhaps I lured her with my charm or my sexiness. My arrogance? Yeah, that makes sense.

"Get in," was all I said, jumping into the driver's side. The windows were still open, so the seats are soaking wet. Damp leather slaps my ass. Fuck it. I did not open her door for her; I assumed she could handle it.

Apparently she can't.

"Open the door Cadence." I growl, leaning over to glance at her. There she is, biting that damn lip again. "Come on just do it. I'm telling you to get in and since you're stalking me, you could at least do what I ask."

"I'm not stalking you." She says but she gets in. She looks like she's about to scream or cry and cut off my head.

Maybe I shouldn't be doing this. Undo everything that both of just said? She doesn't know who she is. I don't know why my heart cratered in when I heard that. She matters to me and I don't want to undo it, even if I don't understand it. Fuck it.

"What are you doing then? If stalking isn't your motive," I ask, glancing at her for half a second. My car seems a lot smaller with the both of us in it. Smashed together, fused but pulling away. Like magnets.

She smells like cinnamon.

Fuck it. “Never mind. Don’t tell me what we’re doing. I’d rather guess. Now I’m starving. Do you like fish?”

I don’t know why I said that. I don’t even like fish. I like Chinese. Pizza. Yeah. This awkward run-in seems like a worthy pizza situation. I swallow, searching my brain for what to say next.

39 I've Been Kidnapped! - Cadence

No, I don't like fish! "Sure. Fish is good." Crap. Crap. Double- and triple-crap. What the hell just happened?

Where am I going with this man?

Does it count as being kidnapped if I willingly got in?

"Fish it is." Mal whispers into the back of his hand. He's rubbed his face in frustration a hundred times since I got in. He signals and turns left, allowing another car to sneak ahead of it. Huh. What a gracious driver he is. I kind of like that. Not that I have any reason to like anything about him. Shut up brain I got this!

40 Invite It In - Mal

Zoey's Fish Palace is non-exclusive. It is centered right behind the garden where Ruth rests. I try not to think about this as I pull in, watching the open sign flash.

The rain has died off and what's followed it is a beautiful peacefulness. The sunlight is glittering off of everything wet. I breathe the scent in, I love it. My lungs feel refreshed. I should be more concerned about driving around with some random woman.

She could be anyone. She could rob me, knock me over the head and take off, but she doesn't. And as we pull up in front of the restaurant I'm blown away by how quiet she is, how nervous she seems.

She plays with her hands, looking only straight ahead. My heart feels full whenever I meet her glance and for some reason I feel my insides start to dance–if only for a second.

My insides quickly still when I remind myself that feeling like this for anyone other than my best friend would be catastrophic. I never want to feel that way again. Love and I are no longer friends; we have no benefits left.

"Let's head in." I silence my engine and unlock my door before hopping out, feeling my back pocket for my wallet. This is an old habit. Ruth used always to tease me about forgetting it.

Cadence swallows and nods, still biting her bottom lip, still playing with her hands. God dammit, she's making me nervous!

She gets out behind me, and I wait on the sidewalk to make sure that she locks the door before closing it. She forgets, so I reach behind her to do it. We get close enough for her to move away and for me to apologize for touching her shoulder with my hand.

She feels solid. Like a real woman.

There is nothing special about my hand on her shoulder, or on her lower back, which is where I now press it.

I guide her towards the entrance to Zoey's Fish Palace. As soon as she pushes the door in all I smell is fish and grease. I watch Cadence duck her head and wonder again what she would like without that orange mop of hair on her hair. Her face is pale but has what looks like about a pound of cover up caked onto it. Whatever, I guess. Her face. Her skin. It's her choice what she wants to smear on it.

Cadence stops ahead of me to nod at the hostess. My hand is still on her back. I don't let myself think about this; I just stop when she stops and start when she starts. She is leading me. I follow her.

The place is small. The walls are glass windows that have been painted over with sharks and other sea creatures.

We sit at a table across from each other. I can see my car from here in the parking lot. I look past her head to a couple holding hands before taking turns holding a tiny tot–a blonde baby thing with a face covered in snot. "Are you going to talk to me or?" Cadence lets her voice die off, looking at the menu with an amusing disinterest. She's still nervous, I can feel it. She's trying to be rude to throw me off.

"If you want to talk, then talk. You're the one showing up wherever I am without rhyme or reason. So what's up? What do I need to know about you Cadence?" I don't look at the menu because I already know what I want. I used to come here a lot. It was a nice place to think and talk.

"I don't know. I've lived here most of my life, and I honestly don't know why I keep showing up where you are. I'm not a stalker, I swear. I just felt like you needed someone who cared. I know that sounds bizarre, but I know what it feels like to be torn apart. I guess I just got the feeling that you've also been there." Cadence crosses her arms, she's looking past me and I can't help but notice how her soft brown eyes are no longer stern.

Is she playing with me I wonder?

"Don't act like you don't know what happened," I warn her, "it was in all of the papers. They had it on every major news network for like a full twenty-four hours. My miserable face has been everywhere. I don't get to be anonymous anymore."

Where is the waitress?

I'm ready to order.

"Have you ever heard the expression, be careful what you wish for?" Cadence is stepping into the tepid water here. I look up at her. Sensing some sort of tension, a nice girl with short hair zips over. I place my order: two chicken burgers and beer. One drink won't hurt. They serve more than fish here. Cadence takes a moment looking the slim pickings over, before swallowing and looking at me for a second longer than she did before.

"Just a diet root beer." She smiles politely, and the girl with the short dark hair disappears without a word.

I silently thank her. As soon as I am alone with this stranger once more the intensity that I felt before once again takes over. A change in the air. It makes me stiffer.

"What? Not hungry?" I probe her.

"I haven't been truly hungry in a long time Malachi." She smiles gently. "Eating to survive is one thing, but eating just because I'm bored and it distracts me is a bad habit that has stuck with me. I have already eaten my weight in chips today, I think it was today. The days all kind of blur together for me." Her soft smile doesn't fade. As if what she just said should be taken lightly but for some reason the words still feel heavy.

"Okay," I say, trying to force the tension away.

It's almost 3:30p.m. I should be headed back home or something, fully prepared to waste the weekend away. Maybe I can catch a movie, sit in the back of the theatre and drink. Sounds like a fine Friday evening to me.

"What are you thinking?" Cadence's sudden question throws me, mostly because it's something that Ruth always used to ask me.

My simple response dies within me. I don't know what to say. The truth? Yeah. Maybe.

"I'm thinking about drinking today and tomorrow and making my night of misery into a beautiful and blurry thing," I explain.

"Why?" Cadence seems upset by something. I don't know why, so I just cross my arms and lean backwards and away.

"Why not?" I say.

"I don't know. Maybe because it's seriously easy to ruin your life that way? I mean I don't mean to come across as judgmental or anything but everything can change in the blink of an eye Mal. One minute your world is peace and butterflies and the next the thing you love the most is being ripped away, and you are the one to blame."

Her words hit home for me.

"Are you speaking from experience Caddie?" I use her nickname without meaning, but she doesn't flinch away.

She just looks at me.

The waitress returns with our drinks, and I thank her politely. Caddie has looked down and away from me; her eyes burning, but she doesn't say anything. She just takes her straw and sticks it in her drink.

I sip my beer and wait.

41 Leave Me Be - Cadence

Why won't he stop looking at me? He is making me want to scream and throw things. Anything and everything.

My manners have up and died apparently. I don't have a lady-like bone in my body. I'm starving, but eating in front of such a gorgeous specimen would only make me want to puke and crawl out of my skin. I can't sit across from him. I can't stand it. This nervousness is making me want to pee my pants. I need to stand and run and never talk to him again.

I can't do any of that. I know I can't.

"If you have something to say then just say it," I demand, stealing his speech from the car and rewording it. His eyes are deep and green and fresh, and they make me mad. Has he always looked this sad? His face looks broken. Will he ever learn to smile again?

Mal just picks up his beer bottle and tips more of the brown liquid back. I have nausea in my stomach. Last night I think I got drunk, I must have. I can't fuck some random guy without a little bit of liquid courage. I feel sick just thinking about it, and I know that I will have to do it all again before the day ends.

Fuck this. I start to stand.

"Never mind, forget that I mentioned any of it. I need to head back, my roommate should be getting home any minute, and I need to check in on him." That's bullshit. I have no idea where Torrance is, and I have no business looking after him. Despite that being the reason that he let me move in, he was lonely and sad. I felt bad. Whatever friendship we had at the time no longer exists, but Mal doesn't need to know that.

"Well I would forget about it, but you know that's not an option. Considering I have no idea what the hell just happened." Mal has apparently decided to be a prick again. Fine, I can handle that.

I stand up to leave him, and the table moves away from my hasty exit. Mal doesn't move an inch. He just takes another slow and careful sip. I have officially had it. I push my hair back and start for the front door, storming right past the pissed off looking hostess.

I don't care about leaving my pop full to the brim, Mal can have it. I trust that he'll pay for it.

The sidewalk outside is still damp. I glare at Mal's cool car and storm past it. My hair is flying in the air. I really should comb it or shave it. Make it nicer, but whatever I'll figure it out later. I head towards the park; the lake always looks awesome this time of year.

I see a headstone that wasn't here before. That's weird, considering this isn't a graveyard.

I start towards the glittery water. I have to cross the parking lot to get there; someone honks at me, and I wave my middle finger. I want to find the source that has drawn me out here, but I don't know where to start. Something deep and embarrassing inside of me wants to find the secret to Mal's heart. I know that no key in my current possession would work.

How did he get so hurt? Why do I care?

His feelings are none of my concern, we all have battle scars. Mine continue to burn as I stalk towards the water. The headstone tells me that I've made it half way there. I have to look at the name because someone is buried here, and it matters. Death always matters. If it were my brother...if he were buried in the earth, I wouldn't want anybody to pass him by with their nose in the air.

Ruthie Jane.

Loving friend.

Daughter,

I will forever wait for us to be together.

Those are some heavy words.

Why did her family bury her here? Alone? Without any other dead souls to talk to or get to know? That sounds twisted, I know. But that is how I picture the after world. A bunch of dead people sitting around a large table, sharing some coffee and a few smokes. Telling stories and jokes. That idea is the only thing that gives me hope; I can barely live with myself now, but I wouldn't be able to at all if I thought for a second that Alex was alone. Wherever he is now, I hope he's surrounded by laughing and joyful fools.

He loved to smile. When we were kids, he used to attack me with water balloons. I would yell at him and send him to his room, but I would give anything for that time back now.

I miss him. He was my home. I have less than nothing now.

42 Where Are You Now? - Mal

I watch Cadence go. I even turn halfway around in my chair to do so, before waving down the waitress and asking for the bill. My food is ready, but I will take it to go. She looks annoyed, so I tip her well. I get up and go, tossing my food into the back seat of my car.

I have lost interest in stalking Cadence now, whatever game she wants to play she can play it by herself. I am done for right now.

The sky is once again a beautiful blue. I keep my windows rolled down and drive towards my house, heading back through downtown. Since it's early none of the weirdos that live in town are out. No one is pounding on car windows begging to be helped out. I'm thankful. Does that make me sound cruel? I honestly don't know. I just hate when people put their hands all over my Chevy™. It's a precious beast you know? A precious beast that I may also like to call Michelle, but that's a secret that not even Ruth knows. Or knew.

Fuck I hate having to talk about her in past tense and all. It screws with my mood. I turn up the radio and tune my thoughts out, looking ahead at the road. Cars weave in and out and I do as well, blinking before I cut off someone but not doing much before cutting off someone else.

I just don't care right now. I don't care at all. About anything at all. It feels terrible.

I don't head home after all because what would be the point in that right now? I decide to head out. I need a night on the town. I have no idea where to go.

I always drink alone, at home in my bedroom or my living room. Playing some first person shooter game or simply watching the sun go down. I'm pathetic. I already know so I do not need to be told. I decide to head to the pool hall. We have one right behind the mall, which is on the south side of Three Hill. We don't have a whole lot of town but the good and the bad sides are divided clearly. A line is practically drawn in the gravel.

I'm on the good side now. The south side hardly has a crime rate at all; the north side is a whole other gong show. Robberies, home invasions and carjackings are a common occurrence.

I never let Ruth cross those tracks. I wanted to protect her until the very end, even if she wasn't always aware of it. She was stubborn and careless. That was one of the things that I hated the most about my best friend. When she was still around that is, I hated her ability to talk herself into any situation, without having a way to talk herself out of it. We talked about it, we fought about it, and she damn well knew how I felt about it, but yet, because she's dead, I feel like I left so much unsaid.

I want to say it. I want to scream it. I feel like I have. Have I gotten through to her yet?

43 Say It Again - Cadence

I hate this town and everything in it. I'm walking in stupid directions at random. I have no idea where I'm headed. I have nothing with me. No purse, no wallet, no cell phone and no jacket. I remember having my wallet at **Walmands**. I hope that I didn't lose it or leave it somewhere random. I will die if it was stolen.

Okay, that was a tad dramatic but you get what I'm saying. My entire life is in that wallet. My favourite photograph of Alex is in that wallet. He was thirteen when I took it at the fair with a cowboy hat hanging off of his head.

He was hilarious. Adorable.

He took my heart with him. I don't know if I'll be ever to get it back or if I'll be the same again. I doubt it.

My parents are fucked up for good. I know that because I saw it happen first hand. A week after my brother's accident, we were told that we should bury him. They wanted us to pull the plug on him. They wanted us to give up on him. They wanted us to stop believing that he would come back again.

A week. That's it. Seven days.

They were heavy worded and short-handed, the nurses, the specialists. I remember only parts of them, random moments. Like having to buy new shoes at the only store open past 5 p.m. because I puked on mine. I was too afraid to see him hooked to machines and lifeless in a hospital bed. The cashier was a total bitch and yet I know that that shouldn't have mattered but it did. There were moments of that week where every part of my existence was in high-def.

I remember the blonde woman who handed me the clear plastic bag with my new shoes in it. She didn't smile, or tell me to have a good day. She just glared and I left. I remember her dimples. Her chin. The way she laughed at me when I left. I was only twenty years old then. Seven years have gone by so fast.

Alex was sixteen. A kid. He wasn't ready for what the world had in store for him, but he should have gotten to experience it. He didn't. I can't help but wonder sometimes if I wouldn't have been born, if Alex has been an only child instead of the youngest, would he still be alive? People always say that when it's your time to go, it's fate. Nothing can change it. I don't believe that. What happened to Alex, it wasn't an accident? It wasn't fate or anything like that. He was trying to protect me, and I failed him.

I was a fuck up back then, even worse than I still am. Hard to believe isn't it? That the current version of me is the good one and yet still, I am a reckless and horrible person.

I hate talking about what happened to Alex. I hate thinking about it because I feel like that makes it fact. I would rather pretend like it didn't happen, but I can't. I hate the fact that me getting shit faced meant him trying to come get me with his best friend. He tried to rescue me alongside Torrance. They were both just kids. Innocent and sweet kids.

Torrance never grew out of that, even though he got the chance. Every day I am so thankful that he did. Get the chance that is.

Alex. Sweet brown eyed Alex. He had sandy blonde hair and a sweet dimpled grin. He was small and always blended in; the girls in town loved him. Actually scratch that, they adored him. Everyone did.

Now seven years have gone by so fast and he's still lifeless on that same fucking hospital bed. He's brain dead and only breathing because we refuse to say goodbye to him. I can't even find the courage to go see him, touch him. I can't stomach seeing my parents or my old friends. What the hell happened?

44 Take Me Back - Mal

The pool hall is crowded. It's also filthy and smells stale. The carpet is sea-foam green. The pool tables closely placed, I watch a smaller dude get elbowed with a pool cue. Laughter and shouting echoes. I feel overwhelmed. I should have expected this, but I didn't. I walk in and head right for the back, pulling out my licence and handing it to the nice chick with the decent sized rack.

She smiles and takes it, asking me what I want. I order beer because fuck it. I don't care what she thought or what anyone else thought. I am a desperate man trapped in a drought. I need refreshment, and I need a lot of it. I see the sweet brunette walk in but don't think much of it. She wonders around the edge of the room, with her hard eyes downcast.

I take a sip. My beer tastes bad but still I swallow it. I sit on a bar stool but give the bartender my back.

I feel like a jackass, like I should be wearing more plaid. Maybe then I would stick out less. I look at the faces that surround me. Faces that laugh and smile before taking a pretty girls hand.

I watch all of this emotionless. Well, almost emotionless. I'm still eye stalking the cute brunette. She doesn't look old enough to be in a place like this. She looks shy and upset. Black cords are hugging her hips. Brown jacket is hanging open. Her top looks like it's made of some clear plastic wrap.

Ugh. Okay then...

I lean back and rest my arm on counter top. All I can think about is Cadence, and I hate it. I hate that I made her mad, but I'm still proud that I did. It was nice to see her react. It was nice to see her brown eyes turn blood red. She smelled of cigarettes and cinnamon.

She couldn't sit still for more than a moment. Right away I noticed that. She was always moving, always playing with her hands, always biting her bottom lip, always looking somewhat sad. I was indifferent to this. Indifferent to her facial expressions and her inner demons. She was just someone I had forced against, she showed up at my house a few times, we've gone out to eat and now that will be that. She can lay whatever sick interest she has in me it to rest. I will not be seeing her again.

45 Lie Against - Cadence

Saturday was awful from beginning to end. I woke up in my bed, for once actually in it instead of you know, just thrown haphazardly on top of it. I blink at my alarm clock. The sun is out; my room is full of it. Someone has been brave enough to push the curtains back, illumining my paper thin walls with the sun's eerie glow.

Was it Torrance? No. he won't come in here again for fear of me becoming possibly unhinged. I don't blame him. I'm scary as hell when I'm mad. I rub the sleep out of my eyes and roll out of bed. I am sure that I look like an ass and I feel like death. There is something gross about my breath. I look around my room and am briefly amazed by the niceness of it. I see neatness where yesterday I saw a mess. My roll-top desk is cleaned off. My eyes graze over the posters pinned up above it. Fan-girl images of movies I used to be obsessed with. I can see my laptop instead of all of the papers surrounding it. Manuscripts I never finished.

I used to enjoy writing; actually that's complete and utter bullshit. I one-hundred-percent totally loved it. I was addicted to it. It made me sick. I dropped it; I killed it and after Alex I could never find the will in myself to pick it up again. It felt pointless. Selfish. How could I enjoy myself when my brother was dead? I would say that I got past feeling like that because I guess in a way I did, but grief is repetitive. It is a tidal wave, ever present but in some moments, more heightened. More intense. You always feel it.

I get up and head towards my closet. I need to get dressed, or re-dressed I guess since I'm still in my red shirt and skin hugging denim pants. They are very hard to sit down in. I have no idea how I slept in them. I see a grey sweatshirt hanging onto a hanger, and I pull on it. The hanger falls into the pits of my closet, and I let it, turning around as I start to strip off my pants. I need to shower, like bad.

I see something silver on the edge of my bed: a Swiss army knife like the kind that Alex used to collect. I have no idea why I have it so close to my bed. That could be seriously dangerous. I hate the part of myself that fears longing to use it, a fear I struggle and push against.

I will not hurt myself again.

I see a pair of camo shorts and pick them out of the overflowing drawer. I know that there's some skanky underwear somewhere in there, but right now I'm just happy to wear a pair of my ex-boyfriend's boxers. I think his name was Mark or Omar? I honestly can't be sure.

I pick up the Swiss army knife and hold it with the blade pointed outwards, crossing my mirror I once again glance at my reflection and my hair. Burnt orange and falling well past my shoulders. I decide to do something that I've never done before. I want to cut my hair. I hold up my bangs and pull the knife backwards, slicing and trimming the hair at an angle that doesn't hurt.

I want short hair. I don't want my looks to matter. I want to be fierce, a true terror. I want everyone on earth to know that Cadence Smalls is here. I will be remembered, for better or worse.

I chop off the back until it is razor short, leaving the front part a little longer as I shape it over. I have a mullet, only backwards. Business in the back, the party in the front. I want the orange gone. I want to bleach and dye my hair and fry it a little more. What could it possibility hurt?

I head out of my bedroom after pulling on my sweatshirt; it's so long that it covers way more than just my boxers. I have yet to pull on my camo shorts. I head downstairs. I know right away that Torrance is here. I can smell his little boy cologne all over. Like *Axe™* and *Old Spice™* mixed. He is trying way too hard. "Do you have a girl over?" I call, listening into the dead air. I think he's in the shower.

Who in the hell is he trying to smell good for?

"Hello? Torrance? I know that you're here so ignoring me isn't going to fucking work." I call over my shoulder before I head downstairs.

We have our own super small basement that is just as creepy as it dark. It's more like a storage dungeon. The floor is little more than dirt with a piece of plywood placed down over top of it. The roof is low hanging; I can't imagine Mal coming down here without hitting his head.

I have to flick on the crappy light halfway down the stairs. It flickers, I have to duck when I reach the bottom and jump over a patch of gross carpet from there. There is literally one square piece of red carpet someone glued to the wood at the base of the stairs.

It smells like mold down here. The walls are fake wood and dark all over, bending with the dampness that hangs in the air. I need to make this quick. I do not want to meander down here. I hurry towards a stack of old hangers and a bunny-eared television that no longer works. There's also a green fridge that I'm terrified to open and the washer and dryer, both of which rest against the far corner.

I know exactly what I'm after. I packed all of my useless shit away down here, all of my nice makeup and concealer. Anything that made me appears prettier and or nicer. I tucked it all away down here to watch it silently burn. I wanted every part of the before to be shattered. My life in the after is a whole different world.

I find the box I'm searching for.

46 With Her - Mal

I took the brunette home after my third or fourth beer. I knew this was a bad idea from beginning to end. I found out her name was Emelia Winters, and she was hoping to get into doing hair full-time, out in the real world. I told her that I totally supported her. I told her I liked the way her thick brown hair rested on her delicate shoulders. Her clear blue eyes looked silver. I lied and said I had never seen anything as beautiful, I kissed her shoulder, stripping her.

And then I fucked her.

God, those are the wrong words. The totally wrong and hurtful words. I did not fuck her. I used her. I brought her home to my townhouse and bent her over after fiercely kissing her. I pulled down her corduroy's and her soft pink underwear. I pulled down my jeans and unleashed my dick on her, forcing her legs apart as she whimpered, aching for more. I sought out her heat and entered her. I didn't even make sure that she was wet enough first. Fuck. My knees are almost crumbled. She was so tight and so God damn warm. Fuck. I pulled out and pushed back in.

Gentler.

Harder.

Faster.

Heavier.

She was bent right over, precious little ass in the air. I reached down to grab her hair and smiled at the sound of my flesh meeting hers. We did not fit well together, but the sweat made us both stickier. This felt like heaven only purer. Real. Warmer. I could grab this girl and touch her. I wanted to do all of this with her until the daylight forced us to start over. I pushed my hands up and under the front of her plastic shirt. It felt like sort of thick rubber. Maybe Emelia was a hipster.

I didn't care. I fucked her harder. I felt the end start when my body convulsed into hers. Fuck. I forgot to wear a rubber. I moaned and said the only name that truly mattered, thank God I said it as a whisper. I'm glad Emelia did not hear because of course; the name was not hers.

It belongs to a stranger. A girl who is no longer here.

She tossed her hair back and tried to push herself off of the armrest of my couch/love chair. I stepped away from her, looking her sweet ass over. She was short and curvy in all the ways that mattered. I pulled up my underwear after grabbing a tissue to clean my dick off, tossing the grossness into the trash.

Emelia turned and looked me over, her dark eyes seeming scattered. She pulled down her shirt and pulled up her underwear.

"Thanks." She said, pushing up at her hair. It was thick and strong, and I wanted to pull it again as I fucked her.

Wait, what was she thanking me for?

"You're welcome." Okay, this was awkward. I had somehow ended up shirtless during this precious and not so precious sudden encounter. I suddenly felt like a dick for bringing her back here. I wanted to show her the door.

"I should probably go home and shower." Emelia wasn't looking me over; she just looked bored. I was anxious and unsure.

"Great. Yes, everyone loves a good shower." I wasn't trying to charm her. She pushed herself fully off of the chair and started back towards the front door. My entire place was pitch dark.

I opened the door for her, breathing in the cold evening air.

My lungs felt sore. My eyes tired. I hid my hand in my pocket and leaned against the door jam, just watching her, waiting for her to say something that I could remember. Instead she just nodded, as if I had just body charged her.

She was ready and warm.

"See you never." She swore. Winking before stepping away and heading towards her car. Had she driven us here?

I suddenly couldn't remember.

I slowly shut the door and leaned against it, hanging my head in the dark. For a moment, I allowed myself to feel despair. Only for a moment because I could not allow my emotions to take over, and once again, I headed upstairs, eager to fall asleep and dream of only her. The only her I was searching for.

47 Suicide Hair - Cadence

I dyed my hair. I actually freaking bleached and dyed my hair. I am currently standing in my bathroom mirror. It's still partially fogged over from Torrance's long ass shower. I know that he's still here because I can hear him opening and closing doors, in a big rush to go nowhere.

"Dude! Get your ass in here and look at my hair!" I squealed and then shut up because embarrassment had taken over. I never made happy noises anymore. I never got excited over my hair. I wasn't that girl.

I looked down at the cluttered bathroom counter until a weary Torrance appeared just over my left shoulder.

I looked up and met greenish blue eyes full of so much hurt and torture. I knew all of it was directed inwards. He was sweet and kind enough to pretend to care about my new hair. Over the years his once youthful face had turned rock hard. His blond surfer hair didn't make him look like a child anymore, his broad shoulders took up every inch of space in the mirror, and he was a mountain over my shoulder.

"Look's good sissy." He smiled, he never smirked. His endearment of talking to me as if I was his older sister was intended to heal–never hurt. But I could not help but flinch at the constant reminder. I was no one's big sister anymore.

"Thanks squirt." I stuck my tongue out at him in the mirror, even though he could never be defined as a squirt, which to me meant tiny and unable to cause harm. Torrance's body begged to differ. He was tall and strong. I could see his muscles under his shirt. I always felt safer when he was here. He could take any intruder with one arm.

I smiled at our reflections in the mirror. At the moment, the deep purple bruises under my eyes and my makeup smudged from the evening prior made me look old enough to be his mother. How had a four-year age different made us so vastly different? I wasn't sure, but I wasn't excited about my new blonde hair anymore.

48 I Know You - Cadence

I left Torrance at home and headed out, grabbing my keys and my favourite coat. I wore my favourite dress that I never had the courage to wear out. I was always scared of standing out, a troll who is trying to play dress up in a hot girl costume. I looked terrible and felt wonderful. How was that possible?

I got into my old beater and turned the radio up to full, in search of something old and beautiful. I did not want powerful right now. I wanted to listen to someone sing about missing another soul. I wanted something real. I wanted to smile. I wanted it to start raining and simply listen to the downpour pound against my windshield, but it's sunny out right now so I just roll the windows down and hit the gas pedal, cruising towards downtown.

Downtown is the divider of the good and the bad side of town. I live in the middle. So like twenty minutes from downtown on a good day without a lot of traffic. The kind of day when I can put the pedal to the metal–kind of like right now. I dream about getting out of this town. I often do. Filling up my gas tank and just hitting the road. It seems simple, it's not. I know. I have bills and responsibilities to other people aside from myself. People that I hope would call and try to track me down.

What if they didn't though? What if they just left me alone? What if I could drive for miles and miles and until the sun fell? All by myself? Singing to the radio. It sounds cool.

I ease on the brake as I cross out of downtown, the pretty part away from the bus depot. Every building is brick and beautiful. Large picture windows abound. Traffic is parked sideways on either side of the road. The thick lines painted yellow. I stayed in the middle lane now, not knowing where and when I would need to turn or if I needed to do so at all. I just wanted to drive until I hit a dead end and was forced to turn around.

I leaned my head back and moved my hand outside of the window, lifting my fingers against the wind's push and pull.

I have never felt nor have I ever been, extraordinarily beautiful. I never worry about someone looking at me and being like "oh wow." I only keep men's attention long enough for whatever we share to become worthwhile. I am an average woman, and I was an even more average looking girl. I am nothing special.

Until I met Mal. I don't even know the dude and somehow he has become everything I think about. When he looks at me, I feel full. Even if the words he's saying are cruel and or unusual. I still feel well. I feel new. I don't know how this is possible. Compared to me Mal is nothing more than a heartless, cruel and fucked up man-child. He's two years younger than Alex would be right now, and that fucks me up more than you will ever know.

I'm twenty-seven. He is barely twenty-two. This cannot and should not be legal and yet I find myself at his door anyhow, knocking nice and loud. I'm biting my lip and willing myself to turn around, but I don't move. I just dance myself into a circle. I left my coat in the car. I push my bangs out. Fuck. He's going to think I look terrible. What grown-ass woman gives a haircut to herself? With a Swiss army knife no doubt?

I feel like a clown and a fool and then he opens the door, and my entire world is turned around and upside down. I don't bother introducing myself. There isn't a point. He already knows me without a doubt. The way his green eyes darken at my approach has me shivering with a suddenly dry throat. I try to swallow. Mal is the only guy I've ever known that could ever be described as beautiful. His cheek bones sharpen as he scowls. Looking down at me through eyes already narrowed.

His shoulders were wide yet I could see his bones. Hallowed and sticking through golden skin that now appeared pale.

He didn't look well, and yet, he looked wonderful. My mind felt torn between the two.

"How are you?" I asked once I was already in his living room. I had to yell seeing as he just totally left me alone.

Smooth.

I take another gander around, my hands on my hips. I slip my feet out of my two-dollar sandals and kick them against the wall. I should have kept them on for an easy getaway, but it just seems rude, even though it seems like Mal's carpet has never been vacuumed.

Who am I to judge though? I haven't put laundry away since I left home. Eons ago.

"I'm great," Mal calls. "Now if you want to be useful, go into my bedroom. Find yourself some clean clothes. I don't care what you borrow just don't touch any of the girls' clothes. Only mine, is that cool with you?"

Girls' clothes? Why does he have girls' clothes?

"Sure." I keep my head down and head towards the dark staircase. Posters line the walls. Movies I've never heard of and books I would never own. Girls in hilarious looking bathing suits.

I know that I don't like Mal at all, but that doesn't mean that I don't want to. I want to be surprised by everything I find and figure out.

I can't believe I'm going into his bedroom.

Oh lord what on earth is that smell? It smells like mold. Or wet clothes that dried in a gross and disgusting pile. Everything smells like a dude. Torrance has never smelled like a gross dude. He keeps his room neat and his clothes, washed, dried and folded. I've never had to bitch him out for not caring about his side of the house. Things are usually the other way around. I'm a slob but even for me, this seems way out of control. I put my hand out to lean against his bedroom wall. His door was wide open instead of tightly closed. It was easy to intrude. This felt normal.

His rug was a deep purple; from what I could see of it anyhow. The ground was covered in clothes and towels. I kicked at a few with my bare toes. I don't know what I expected to find or do.

I wasn't stripping in here. No way, no how.

Still though, my mind clouded with doubt. I looked back down. I needed to change into something comfortable. I wanted to make myself useful before Mal kicked me out. I wanted to be in control; I wanted to feel normal.

I wanted to laugh. For some reason I felt like I could laugh a lot around Mal, I hadn't felt that way in a while.

Even though he was as cuddly as a cold, electricity flooded pole, I still wanted to get close. I wanted to feel. What better way to warm me into his tight little bubble? I picked up a shirt off of his bed post, feeling the soft material and lifting the fabric up against my nose. I inhaled.

Wow. Whoa.

Memories blurred in the back of my head like I had shaken a snow globe. Soft and cold. I knew right away that these memories were not my own but still, I couldn't help but feel overwhelmed.

I saw Mal. I saw him the way he was now and the way he must have been months if not years ago. I saw him so happy that he had glowed before his eyes became overshadowed, and he once again became miserable. I saw him looking at me like I hung the moon and felt his body curving against mine within the snow. He was my warmth in a cold and cruel world.

I saw him smile his smug smile and felt my insides twirl. I felt him controlling my every mood and sentence without having to try at all. I saw him making me cry when he didn't pick up my hundred-and-forty-two calls. He sent me straight to voicemail.

I felt it all. I felt myself being let down and pulled back up only to be thrown over a waterfall. I felt myself drown. I felt myself let go.

I drop the shirt back onto the ground, stepping back. No longer being careful I bump into his dresser and knock over a lamp and a bottle of very girly looking perfume or cologne. Honestly, who the fuck knows.

I just want to bolt.

"Hey now, slow down." Mal almost smiles. My entire body set ablaze by his tone. I whirl around, but he has both arms out, keeping me safe from the rest of his breakable shit.

My back is against his chest. One ab is pressed against my lower back, and I can't think with him manhandling me like this. "Stop that," I demand, or at I am least trying to, but I can't say much of anything with him looking at me like he is, like he wants to laugh because I'm such a spaz–or kiss my eyelids.

Fuck. I did not just think that.

"I can't stop anything if I don't know what I did." Mal's voice was suddenly heated. We were almost the same height when he was all leaned over like that. His lips are brushing my nose. I breathed him in because I simply couldn't help it and I all I got was frost on my skin.

The snow globe had invaded into my personal business. I couldn't make sense of it.

"You touched me," I told him, "and you snuck up behind me like some creepy-ass cat. I hate when people do that. Announce your presence, tie a ball around your neck."

I did not just say that. What the heck?

Mal laughed. Full on smiled and laughed. His eyes crinkled, and he looked so handsome right then I wanted to eat him.

I looked down and stepped away from him.

"I'm going to wear this, and that." I picked up the smelly shirt a pair of what looked like jogging pants. "You cool with that?"

Mal nodded.

"Then move your ass and let's get to it."

49 Back Together - Mal

I woke up on Sunday after having dreamt of only her green hair, brown eyes, soft and hard words, all of it mixed together.

I woke up hurt.

I was still shirtless, half covered by a duvet that hadn't been washed since forever. The hot sun fucking hurt, I tried to roll over but my muscles ached, and I wanted to vomit all over.

I felt somewhat sober. Awake. Alert. My vision did not blur.

Okay. This was weird. I get up and once again head for the shower, stripping off my underwear on the way there. I glance at myself in the bathroom mirror. My emo hair. My green eyes.

My body that the girl went all weak in the knees for. What do they see in me? The girls I sleep with I mean.

What do they see that makes them want me? Is it that obvious that I have money? If it is something about me is lying. My family has money, it's not mine. Whatever I take is only borrowing. In reality, I have nothing worth giving. I look away from my face, turning slowly away. I don't want to look at myself today. I kick back the shower curtain. I turn the water to a spray and jump into the tub haphazardly. The water hits me in the face. I close my eyes; it feels like ice. It stings.

I start washing, reaching down for a bottle of soap that needs to be filled up. I slather my chest, my arms. Washing and scrubbing and rubbing. I harden at the memory of what I was dreaming.

Flo pressed against me, begging for me to stay.

I'm disgusting. Repulsive really. Flo would totally roll her eyes at me.

Can you hear me Ruthie? I hear you always. I hear you thinking and breathing even if it's just a memory. I hold you with me. I need you with me. Remembering you is like breathing. I feel your hand holding mine, and it doesn't feel like a dream. Not really.

It feels real in all of the ways that holding you could be. Like somehow you are here, you are touching me. It doesn't feel like you're alive but somehow in between maybe? Like you've battled against space and time to get back to me. Would you ever do such a thing? Maybe.

I rinse my body, bringing myself into a pathetic ecstasy before washing all the evidence of self-satisfaction away. That is all that I get nowadays. I head downstairs after showering because I'm starving. I open the fridge and frown when I find it empty. I should not be surprised. I hate buying groceries. I usually pick up enough to get me through a few days at a time. I guess I know where I'm headed today.

I pulled on a pair of pants with a draw string waist. I don't tie it tight. I'm shirtless in the hot sunlight, yet I still find myself shivering. Somethings feel different and strange about today. I don't know why.

I look around me. Nothing is moving. My kitchen looks the same, bland and boring. My tan kitchen cupboards are all closed, hiding messes but looking a lot nicer than they did last night. As if someone attempted to tidy up the place. Okay, maybe something does look strange.

I'm not an all-out slob by any means, but I am also not an insane neat freak. I've never liked cleaning, that was Flo's thing (when she was PMSing at least, only when she was PMSing). It was as if she could work her frustration away. The counters are halfway decent; I must have done it in some drunken state. Yeah, that almost makes sense.

I pick up a half empty can of pop and take a drink before rearranging my face. It tastes disgusting. I pour what's left into the sink and wash it away before tossing the can into the recycling. I have the sudden urge to clean. This scares me. I don't know how to clean. I have no idea where to start or what must take place for me to do such a thing. I know this makes me sound like such a guy, but my mom never made me clean.

She did everything for me, which is why I moved out and tried to run away. So many times, I just wanted to be free. I wanted to think for me. I wanted to make myself happy and bring myself the misery. I was sick of my mother delivering it for me. I turn on the sink, grabbing a clean dishrag out of the drawer; I start to clean, scrubbing the counters and the back-splash leaving soapiness behind me.

I love lemon scented things.

I move some dirty plates out of the sink after scrubbing them clean with the pre-used soapy dishrag. The thought of spreading bacteria of some kind vaguely occurs to me, but I don't give the thought much time.

I keep wiping. Cleaning. Scrubbing.

Singing. I can't remember the last time that I did this. sang out loud into the silence without any accompanying music and lyrics. I just like the feel of it. I also like the sound of it. I sing for Flo and for what we have. I feel almost okay for a moment before I allow the terror to seep back in. Are these the only kind of moments that I will ever get? Fleeting happiness? Will my life ever feel normal again? Will I ever be able to withstand the wind?

Memories and moments are threatening to break in. It's only when I notice that an actual person is trying to get in that I realize I'm dancing half naked in my kitchen as I put away my dishes.

"Keep your pants on!" I threaten, making my way to the back door in the living room. I have such an ass-backwards townhouse.

It is home though.

I plod barefoot into the living room. I look around; I look at the couch covered in pillows, my dusty television and the remote. Fuck I need to vacuum and take the garbage out. I made a list of other mundane and normal things I need to do before unlocking the deadbolt. I pull open the door and feel something inside me move.

I know the woman that I'm looking at right now, only I don't because now her once burnt orange hair has formed a sort of halo. It is glowing and gold. Hanging over her face, the ends perfectly gelled and styled. She wears a dress covered in skulls.

She doesn't move.

I exhale.

"Good morning Cadence, how can I help you?" I'm being polite because I know that there isn't a point in being rude.

I'm not a total asshole. Only when I'm in a mood. I feel okay right now. "I need to talk to you," she barges right past me into my living room, eyeing the arm that I have extended out. She's totally eye-fucking my muscles. I grin without meaning to and feel insanely proud for like a moment or two. Yeah, I used to work out. Key words being used too. Lately I've been too sad and lazy to even move, my body has kept up nicely though.

"So talk. I'm not stopping you." I cross my arms and turn around, my eyes groping her ass. It is perfectly round and sticking out. The fabric of her dress clinging to her skin, I cringe before adjusting myself. Cadence has her back to me while inspecting my place and checking behind the couch. I think she's making sure that no one else is home. She probably doesn't know that I live alone.

I chuckle.

"I had a dream about you only I wasn't asleep, and it freaked me out," she turns around. "Don't do that. Don't look at me like I'm some crazy girl that just wants to sleep with you. You're a child in my eyes, Mal. A twenty-something child who doesn't know how to take care of himself. It would be so easy for me to hate you and to be disgusted with you without even knowing you, but I'm not and I don't and it's freaking me out. I woke up one day and needed to see you even though I didn't know you, and now I'm walking around town dreaming about you."

Cadence's voice has dropped to a sexy low. Looking at her like this, all upset and freaked out makes me want to growl. I feel like an animal.

"What did you dream about?"

"I don't know. I just saw you. All of you. Naked and up close and you can't even try to make me fuck off by saying I'm fantasizing about you because it felt so real. I could feel you."

I felt her too. I can feel her now when we're steps apart, and I could feel her when I saw her through that store window. It more than freaked me out.

"That's cool." I drag the words out because I don't know what to do. I want the door closed but I feel like the heat in my body might make all of the windows explode. "So what? Do you want to hang out? I was just about to clean house. You can join me if you want to, but I don't have any food. I'm all out, and I'm broke. So murdering me and robbing me is also off the table. Just so you know."

I laugh when Cadence calls me "an asshole," but she doesn't run out. This also makes me smile before I frown. I feel like I'm getting in over my head now.

I hate how I find her beautiful and wild. With her hair lighter and cut down, I can see her whole face now. Her full cheeks and lips are puffed out from being chewed. Brown eyes like melted gold. Like the colours of the woods in the fall.

Her chest is pushed out as she breathes in and out. Angry and nervous in all in one go. I get under her skin. I know. I don't know why though.

"I'll help you." Cadence looks down, voice dropping in what must be the sexiest way possible. Her eyes touch my skin, sending chills right down to my bones. Every time she moves closer it's like a physical stroke.

Fuck. I growl. I'm totally ashamed of myself right now. I feel like an animal. All I want to do is grab Cadence and roll her onto the ground, spreading those curvy legs out.

I swallow. I've been staring at Cadence for a good minute-and-a-half now, and she still hasn't decided to bolt.

I should stop screwing around.

"Well if you want to help out I'm not going to stop you, but you can't clean in a dress like that unless you don't plan on bending down," I let my new friend know with a smile. I close the door behind her and lock the dead bolt before turning back around.

I leave Cadence in my living room. I hope she follows.

50 What the Fuck Was That? - Mal

Hello universe, me again. Just wondering what on earth I did to deserve this? I've got a woman cleaning my house and dusting my fake plants, while I rearrange my television.

Wouldn't it be easier if she were in my bed? Why couldn't you just do that? I just want to fuck Cadence and get her over with. I want her out of my head. I want whatever I felt while she was pressed up against my chest to flutter off and pretend to be dead. I can't take this.

Having her in my arms, I felt something that made me angry and mad and sad and every other emotion one can come up with.

I felt like I'd come home again.

I felt alive, and I felt dead.

I hadn't felt this much hatred for anyone since I lost my best friend. Hating Ruth had been expected. That's what all the grief councillors said, I was supposed to hate her for leaving and find a way to forgive her. I was supposed to understand that she did what she did because she saw no other option. She was sick, depressed. Manic.

I miss her like I would miss my head if it rolled off and into the sand. I miss her the way I miss warm clothes right out of the dryer. I ache for warmth, and I ache for her. I miss everything about her. My memories of her aren't even memories anymore. They feel like a DVD I keep trying to start over. She hasn't been gone that long, and yet it feels like forever. With Cadence here all I can feel is the anger but still I allowed myself to laugh at her instead of with her. I need to try harder to hurt her.

I look over. Cadence is bent over, I almost growl and have to hide my face in my elbow to stop my smirk.

She looks so damn good in my shirt. The shorts she chose to hug her every curve. They are spandex running pants that I have never worn. Spandex is just not my thing. I don't need to display my junk for the world.

Is it weird that I want to display my junk to her? Yeah. That is totally fucking weird. I need to stop staring at her. I need to get my act together. I need to stop washing the same part of the wall over and over. I've cleaned it at least nine times by now.

"Do you smoke in here Mal? Or did you, I don't know. Used to? Everything is yellow. When I was little, my grandma smoked four packs a day in the house while she watched TV." Cadence picks up a half empty chip bowl and turns around, warming me up with her golden eyes. Her soft lips move, forming a small frown. She stops herself from letting me see her small smile.

I see the ghost of it anyhow. It makes her look vulnerable, much younger than she is right now, as if we're on the same playing field.

"She was mean, but she had a quick mind. She remembered everything; she knew everyone's names and she memorized birthdays. She died when she was like eighty-nine, but her brain was still like lightning." She has stopped pruning my fake tree long enough to smile at me.

"Anyway her whole place had to be stripped after she died, she ruined the paint and the flooring. The window coverings, everything, was yellowed with nicotine. It was kind of disgusting but hilarious at the same time. It was like her getting the last word for the last time. She was dead and at peace, and we were all stuck cleaning."

I watch her face glow at the strange memory.

"My brother Alex liked to clean. He was odd that way. One time in like grade twelve or something, I skipped class and came home early only to find him singing, cleaning and making lemonade." Cadence turns to face away from me, her words hanging.

"I'm sorry." I say because it's better than saying nothing.

"What happened to your brother Caddie?"

51 "What Happened to Your Brother Caddie?" - Cadence

It was such a simply question that Mal asked me. One that shouldn't have made my face rush with heat. I shouldn't have dropped the plant I was just dusting, but I did anyway. It hit the carpet and rolled away, sideways.

I couldn't say anything.

My mouth felt suddenly flimsy, my chest ached, and I looked around helplessly for someone or something to rescue me. I had ruined everything quite easily.

My life had never been cake. It has always been messy. Our parents fought about the little things constantly. About every little hair out of place. The mismatched cutlery. Everything. Constantly.

Alex and I wanted to escape that day. He was sixteen and so sweet and innocent. Dark hair and clean blue eyes. Charming to anyone who looked his way. He had me wrapped around his pinkie before his first birthday. I had heard about a party; I had begged him to come with me. He said he hated me drinking. I went anyway, and the rest is history.

"My brother died because of me." I hear myself saying suddenly. Waiting for the second bomb to drop but Mal just looks at me, waiting expectantly and carelessly. I know that deep down, there's no way that he is interested by anything I say, and yet for some reason, he seems unable to look away. The tension between us is so thick you could cut it and serve it to three, pretending that it was leftover birthday cake. I want to lick the frosting. I want to lick Mal. God, I am crazy sounding.

"He died because of me," I say, explaining what I said already, repeating myself out loud and in my brain. "He's lifeless right now on a hospital bed, he would be pronounced dead if we unplugged him. He can't breathe on his own, he has no brain activity. His organs are failing constantly."

"It's all because of me. I was a moron. I went out drinking with some buddies, and I had to call my little brother to rescue me, that's awful, right? He was only sixteen but he called his friend, and he and Torrance headed for me straight away." My stomach is churning. Dancing and spinning. I feel like I've been drinking.

"I was on the couch alone and some guy started undressing me. He said that he got the wrong idea when we were dancing, and that I had to be punished. So like I said, I called Alex and Torrance. At least I kind of remember it like that." I swallow the memory like my throat is full of venom. My body stiff as that creep pushed his cock against it, his breath felt hot, and I felt sick.

He got me on my back in no time flat.

"I cried for them like six or seven times while it was happening and suddenly they burst right in, two heroes looking for worship even though they were just kids. Alex was good at being scary when he was mad, and he got so furious when he saw what had happened. He picked me up like I weighed nothing and carried me out my parent's van. He had borrowed it I guess, more room for drunk me to lay in."

"I couldn't stop crying," I continued "and I remember Torrance looking over at Alex when they jumped into the front, he said, 'are we just going to let him get away with that?' And Alex nodded. I was so relieved when I saw this. They were just kids; I should have fought my battles instead of relying on them, but I always did. We didn't make it home, but I'm sure you've already guessed that. I don't even know exactly where we were when it happened, when some moron crossed the center line, and we crashed straight on into him."

"Alex was dead. Before I even knew what had happened, Alex was dead, but they tried to revive him and they did for like half a second. They transported him by air ambulance to Calgary, and Torrance was so numb and sick and I just felt lifeless. I woke up in a hospital bed and I knew that my life would never be the same again. I knew that nothing would ever matter again, and I was almost okay with that, because I wanted to be dead. I wanted to trade spots with Alex." I swallow, avoiding looking directly at him. Mal, his precious is pushing against my chest.

He takes a step forward; I take two back.

"I don't deserve to live." A million times I have said this and every single time I meant it. I'm not looking for pity, only an acknowledgement of my regret. My fucked up life choices.

I did this, I ruined my life. I changed the stars and didn't mean to do it. Alex should have lived.

He should have had the chance for his first and last kiss, he should have seen the sun rise every morning, and he deserved to feel it. He was such a good kid. I loved him more than words understand, and I know that never again will I love another like that.

"What do you deserve then?" Mal asks, he has gotten into my space without being noticed. He reaches out for me, and I fight the urge to slap him. I don't know what will happen when I am once again touched by him. I blink and look up at him. His eyes are flat, his voice heavy and grief tinged.

"This," I say without an explanation, and I kiss him. I have to stand on my tip toes to reach him. My hands latch onto the back of his neck, I try to angle my mouth against his as he stiffens.

"Cadence..."

"No, don't ruin it."

His lips are warm and rough, I know right away that his world is no safe haven. My nose pushes against his, I devour his sullen lips. Pushing and silently pleading with him to pull back for whatever I've taken.

Mal stays still. His hands in raging fists at his sides. Still, I kiss him.

I graze his bottom lip with my tongue, nipping the pink skin until he trembles. I want so badly for him to kiss me back. I pull back to look at him, his green eyes are hooded.

"Jesus, you can really kill a girl's confidence." I play with him, touching his bare chest. "I thought I was good at this, that's what all of my ex-boyfriends..." he cuts my words off and growls as if he hates the taste of them. His hot mouth pressing against my lips until I open for him.

He moves when I move. He tastes like heaven. Whisky and something sweet and solid. It burns when I kiss him.

I let it.

52 I Like This - Mal

I like this. I clench my fists and lean in, Cadence's mouth is abrasive at first kiss. Her touch persistent, I lean into her.

Letting her work at my closed lips, she's giving me chicken kisses. The texture of her lips becomes velvet as I laugh, before I kiss her back a little bit. Opening my lips, allowing her entrance as I grab her arms, bending in half to back her up.

Our tongues do a strange dance, all I can feel is wetness and we both laugh. She has her hands on the back of my head.

This is awkward as all shit, pulling me even further in. She keeps giving me chicken kisses, pecking at my face with her lips.

I grin. I want to touch her ass. I've always been an ass man; my fingers ache with the need of her skin. I want to reel her in, I never want to let anyone get close to me again, and I never want us to exist without the other in our strange little orbit. For right now, I just like this.

"What are we doing?" I don't need to ask, I've gotten a pretty good idea as to what we're doing and where this is headed. My bed, with her bent over it. Yeah, I can picture that.

"Kissing," Cadence says.

I feel her happiness. I don't know if I like it, I'm a bit creeped out by it. The light in her eyes? That's not for me. I know it.

She must have some other dreamboat locked up in that funny head. I reach up to cup her chin, tilting her head back, my thumb tracing her raw bottom lip, while my other hand strokes my way down her back, towards the curve of her ass.

She's fucking my mouth into oblivion. Our breathing heavy, I move my lips to her jaw, her neck, sucking and biting her pink flesh. She whimpers, waking up my dick.

My boner is officially awakened.

I should have let her wear that stupid dress. It would have made everything a lot more convenient. My hands trace the fabric of my pants that have stretched over her skin. I go back to bite her bottom lip before slipping my hand into the back. Hand on her ass. Flesh on flesh. I give her skin a little slap. When Cadence perks up a bit I know that she enjoyed it. She pulls back.

"What?" I ask.

"Nothing," she says. "That was just..."

Awesome, sexy as all shit?

"...ugh different?" Cadence finishes. Eyes heavy lidded.

She kisses me again.

It's a closed lip kiss. We peck at each other like idiots. I slide my hand further down her ass, grabbing warm flesh. She cries against my lips and gasps. I want all of her skin.

I drop my other hand from her chin and push down her borrowed shorts. The elastic band slaps her hips, so I rub the reddened flesh as Cadence sucks on my bottom lip. I feel like I'm eating her face, but I'm also enjoying it. My fingers are seeking her entrance.

I find her heat, her folds hot and wet, waiting for my fingertips. I dip right in, circling her clit. Cadence moans and arches her back. I feel like she's never been touched like this. I feel like this is strangely intimate.

I swirl the tip of my finger against her entrance. Pushing in, Cadence silently begs for my other hand. I give right in. She spreads her thighs and pushes down on my wrist. We have barely moved an inch.

"Say it." I headily demand. Looking into her face and wishing that she would keep her eyes wide open.

"Tell me the truth, as you ride my hand. Say you came over here for sex, tell me that you're a whore and a stupid little bitch. Say that this is all you wanted. Say that you just want me out of your head. Tell me that I'm imagining the relief I feel whenever you brush against my skin."

I cup her warmth in the palm of my hand. She whimpers again. My pointer finger traces circles against her entrance, my thumb petting her hot skin. She's like velvet, and she can't seem to get enough of my hand.

"Say it."

A breathy moan escapes her pink lips.

"Say it, Cadence. Say that all that being drawn to me stuff you said was bullshit. Say that you're just a whore looking for attention. Tell me the truth, come on baby say it, say you didn't mean it." My words betray my emotions. The hate I'm feeling is purely selfish.

She tightens under my hand. Her shoulders are pulling in until we are pressed chest to chest. She's panting, and I'm exhausted. My entire body floods with some strange emotion when she breathes into my neck, my fingers still brushing against her tender skin. Her words are a mixture of daylight tainted with darkness.

"But I did mean it...."

53 But I Did - Cadence

I fucked Mal's hand. I fucked a stranger's hand, who the hell does that? Oh right, this chick. This fucked up and demented chick.

This is one of the many moments where I wish that I was still a virgin because I know that if I were a virgin, what I expect to happen now wouldn't be expected. Maybe if this was my first time with a man I'd have hope that it would happen again, but I know enough to know that that's bullshit. He's going to leave me like this, I know it. I'm not innocent or naive. I'm not an idiot.

I look up at Mal and wait for him to remove his hand. His thumb still brushing my trembling flesh. Surely he must want to wash and sanitize it. His hand that is.

I try not to close my eyes against all of the things that he just said. He called me a little bitch, a whore. He pleaded with me to tell him that our fading connection was only in his head, my heart squeezed at the realization that he also felt it. I sucked in a breath before letting my thoughts scatter again.

He doesn't want this to be more than it is. He wants to work us out of each others' subconscious. It shouldn't upset me but it does, and he did.

"Are you okay Cadence?" My new friend asks. He's looking at me with such a strange tint to his evilness. His hand is still buried in my sex. He teases me with his finger prints.

I wish for the smirk on his face to be ever present. I love the Cheshire Cat, smug look to him, as if I'm Alice and we just stumbled into Wonderland, lost and delirious. Is that what this is?

But he just stares. And I stare back.

What just happened? I need to ask; I need space away from him. I long for a second loss of contact. The heat his body gives is too much. I'm burning up with it. "Why did you do that?" my voice is breathless. *Why did you touch me like you just did? Push me towards the brink of existence while I begged for it.* I know before I even ask my question, the answer that he's about to spit back. He doesn't sound breathless.

"Because you asked for it?"

Did I?

"I didn't." I tell him.

Just like that his smirk is back, I blush. My sudden embarrassment warming up my face and neck, his cockiness spurs butterflies in my stomach.

I'm humiliated. I hate this. I need distance. I crave it.

I'm still dressed but I feel exposed and naked. He finally removes his hand. I feel hot, uncomfortable. I ache for him to touch me again.

I suddenly hate myself for forgetting to put on underpants. I wasn't wearing any when I showed up in that stupid dress; I'm such a slut I can't stand it. I did come over for this. my subconscious needed it. Fuck, I hate thinking that because when my face drops, I know that Mal notices. My brain empties for fear that he can read it. He's so God damn good with his hands; I wouldn't be surprised if he were a magician.

I did not just think that.

But I did.

"Something wrong, Cadence?" he removes himself from my tiny little bubble of a sad existence and struts back, running his hands through his messy black tresses. Fuck I want to do that.

"Yeah, I need to change. I need to head home. I shouldn't have done that. It was..." what it was, was awesome. Beyond my greatest expectation of a sexual experience.

"It was odd," I conclude and silently wait for Mal's smug face to drop, but it doesn't. He's so bloody handsome that I fucking hate it. It makes me nervous and not able to look at him.

I'm not shy. Not in the slightest. Considering I just rode his hand like a queen I should strut out of this place as if it was a mansion, but I can't even find my tongue. My palms have started to sweat, and I feel so awkward standing here in his clothes. I feel self-conscious. When the fuck did that happen?

Mal laughs a good old belly laugh while he opens his fridge only to scowl at its emptiness before closing it. He stops at his sink to wash his hands, smirking at me when he switches on the faucet.

"It wasn't odd Cadence, and you know it. It was way beyond that, but I'm not going to argue with you about it, at least not right now. I'm not going to fight with you, because I don't have time for that." He finishes washing his hands, and I still find myself unable to move away from him. I look down at the pants he easily slid his touch in. I do a squat to rearrange them so that I can cover up my lady business. I don't need Mal seeing any more of it.

"I have to finish cleaning and then I've got to head to the store, grab some stuff. Groceries and whatnot. You can come if you want."

I already *came* you eggnog. All over your stupid hand. "I want to come with."

"Good, get cleaned up."

Oh, I'll get cleaned up, you moron. He finishes washing his hands for a good twenty minutes before he shakes the excess water off, spraying me with it as he reaches for a tea towel to dry his skin.

I just watch him, just like a total drugged up love sick puppy dog/ moron. Oh yeah, that totally happened.

No, regrets. Ha. Do you get it? God, that movie was brilliant.

I snap the elastic on my borrowed shorts/pants (because for some reason I want to call them pants) and head upstairs to retrieve my dress. I barely get up the stairs before I've pulled Mal's shirt over my head and tossed it onto his mattress.

I hung my dress on the door to his closet because I didn't want to wrinkle it. I unhang it, pulling it in front of my dress and glancing into the mirror at it. I love this dress, and I hate it. I hate that wearing it earns me male attention. I know that I deserve it, all of Three Hill knows my sordid past. I made sure of that when I went out to the bar on every available occasion. When I'm drunk, I like to talk about Alex, I can't help it. It just happens.

I decide not to pull on my dress, and instead, decide to delve further into Mal's closet–looking for the skeletons I know he has. I push it open; it is built with the kind of doors that bend. They're nice and wooden. I smooth my knuckles over the wood and breathe in. All I can see is shirt sleeves and darkness. I take a step in and totally know how bad this is, how mad I'm sure Mal will be at me if I get busted. This doesn't stop me, though. I keep right on snooping. The first item I grab is a blue dress shirt with lots of creases that desperately need to be ironed out of it.

I've never had the urge before but suddenly I am possessed by it. Oh crap, I have to bite my lip to stop from fulfilling that death wish. Silently wondering why my vagina is being so overactive.

I've never before wanted to act like such a typical and stereotypical house wife/1950's model citizen (woman).

Blag. Gross. Get it out of my head!

The next item I find is a suit, a black one, with a nice blue tie hanging loosely around it. It's nice, but something about it fills my entire body with dread. I feel sick, and not just because of what Mal and I just did.

I touch the sleeve of the suit jacket. It's the kind of suit one buys from some expensive tailor and only wears it once. For a wedding or a graduation...a funeral even. I try to swallow as I think this. My brain fighting not to process it. I try to blink it all away the moment that I remember it, the service. Not Alex's. Someone else's. A service Mal showed up to in this suit. I don't know how I picture it but the memories come like puzzle pieces. It was awful from beginning to end. A crap load of tears and sad music. I think that they even played some sad **Disney™** music during it. Elton John's voice is banging on my head.

I drop the suit jacket from my grasp and try to step back, shaking my now throbbing head. What happened?

Whose casket was that?

I know damn well none of it belonged to Alex, so why am I remembering moments from a time I wasn't present? I do not just remember all of it, I'm feeling it.

"Cadence?" I hear his voice before his careful steps, I know that if I look over my shoulder I'll find him, but I can't do that.

I close my eyes and turn away from him. "Yeah, I'll be right down. Just need to pull on my dress. It's a tight fit."

Why on earth did I say that? As if Mal needed to be reminded that I'm fat.

"So don't wear it," he simply says, stepping towards me. His eyes are on his open closet. He reaches into it without questioning why I opened it.

"Here. Take this." Mal says, handing me a large white t-shirt long enough for me to wear as a dress. I grin. I can't help it, quick to rearrange my face before Mal can notice.

He just grunts in confusion. I kind of like that about him.

"Change into a pair of my sweats, they won't cling to you as much and I don't want any other dudes seeing your ass while we're out in public." He pulls them off of my skin and snaps them back; I do a little "that kind of hurt, but I liked it" dance.

Again, he just grunts in confusion. I smile like an idiot.

I am beyond okay with Mal saying he doesn't want anyone being able to see my ass while I'm with him. I should be beyond offended. My assets should equal *only* my business. He should have no say in how I dress.

So why does he all of a sudden?

"Hey! Wait a minute." I pull his shirt over my head. "Why did you say that? Why do you care who looks at my ass?" My words are somewhat muffled by the fabric, but I think Mal got the most of it.

He shrugs and even that look on him is delicious, as much as I hate to say it.

"What?" I demand,

He grunts again and heads downstairs. I growl and follow behind him after changing into a pair of black sweats I found on his bed.

Somehow they fit.

I have to step over meaningless items to keep from tripping and ending up on my head; his staircase is just as bad. Mal doesn't seem to act like he notices, even if he does, he's gotten good at descending through the chaos. I'm careful and super slow at it, holding on to the railing like I want to baby it, and rub it, which I am at the moment.

This gets more sexual the more I think about it. I look at the back of Mal's head and pretend that I want to kick it. He's got such a nice head, and beautiful shoulders to match. I love hi–

Fuck. No. I did not just think that. That did not just happen. I shake my head and attempt to sabotage any and all remnants of it. That horrible almost sentence. Yuck. Nope. I want no part in it, any of it.

I don't do feelings or false expectations. Romance and I are not friends. Soulmates? Fate? Fuck all of that. I don't believe in any of it. If it's true, I demand evidence. I just can't see the goodness in being meant for only one person.

What if that person ends up dead? Or you end up dead? Are you just going to claw your way out of heaven to get to them? How would you even do that? My body floods with a strange sadness but I ignore it.

I have once again reached Mal's kitchen.

He stops in the middle of it to pick up his wallet. I follow him once again, like a total love sick puppy.

He seems to accept this.

"Where are we going?"

"Probably just to **Walmands**. That's like the only place open after six on a weekend. You know how this town is."

I did.

He opened the door located in his kitchen and stepped out of it, nodding his head for me to follow his exit.

I did.

He reached behind me to lock up and somehow ended up slapping my ass, again. I knew enough just to roll with it. The sun was still at work trying to burn any and all humans trying to stay alive beneath it, the heat slipping into my skin and under it. I really shouldn't have worn a black bra with this outfit, you can totally see it through the thin white fabric of my shirt.

Everyone's looking. Women and men. I feel like Julia Roberts in the hooker movie. I'm both being objectified and looked down on and getting no enjoyment whatsoever out of it. This feels like a pretty awkward and shitty situation, maybe this is happening because I'm strutting behind Mal like a tramp and the parking lot in front of his townhouse is flooded with neighbours and fellow students.

Mal unlocks his Chevy™ when we get up close to it. I shiver in the sun and look over the roof at him. He's perfect. Moody and gorgeous, mean and cruel. Hot-headed.

How do I all know all of this? How do I feel it? I don't fucking get it.

"What's your absolute favourite radio station?" Mal asks as we get in. I close my door and look anywhere but at him. His car feels way to small with both of us squished into it.

My elbow touches his. I feel gigantic. Awkward and fucking fantastic.

"98.5 FM," I tell him. "They play all the good stuff. The soft pop and angry chick music. I love it."

"Angry chick music, what the hell is that? Some kind of Taylor Swift shit?" Mal looks at me, and I look back at him.

He so deserves a good smack.

"Well yes, but she's the queen of everything, so I'm just going to pretend that you didn't say that. I love angry chick music; I love anything beautiful born out of aggression. A break up is awesome because of the emotions triggered by it."

Every bit of pain has some beauty built into it. I one-hundred-percent believe this. But still, I go up and down with it.

I know every route to **Walmands**: the back roads and the main ones, the busier streets and the dead and empty ones. I have pretty much lived in the junk food section since Alex. Sour gummy worms are my favourite. I also like sour cherries. If you wanted to you know, make a note or something out of that.

Mal switches to my favourite radio station and just like that angels all out the heavens. "Renegade" by **Lorraine** is playing, and I'm totally in love with it! *You take a part of my heart/ you pull it away/ I know we will both be better if it breaks.* I belt these beautiful words out of the window, turning around to look expectantly at Mal, again. He just grunts, feigning being confused.

I don't want to stay away/be my renegade.

My dance moves are awesome so that you know. *You dance with me under the street lights/ this is our masquerade/ be my renegade.*

I scream and totally fall out of tune. Mal almost smiles, almost. That almost counts.

I reach over to turn the music down, listening to Justin swoon me in the background. My heart is beating super swell for that dude right now. Also, you know, kind of for Mal. At least a little. Don't tell him or I'll kill you.

"Why do you even listen to the radio? Why don't you just plug in your iPhone?" I for some reason want to know.

"I don't know," shrugs Mal. "I kind of like to think that every song that I've download onto my phone holds a memory that I don't like to talk about. Listening to those songs makes it almost too real."

Makes what almost too real?

"Flo?" the name leaves my mouth and I have no idea what to do. I'm confused. I didn't think we were talking about water or my menstrual cycle, but you never know. Yeah. I'm gross. I know.

I wasn't afraid of Mal's driving skills before now. He slams on the breaks, and since I forgot to put on my seatbelt I fly towards the windshield, holding my hands out to defend myself.

"What the fuck dude?" I bellow.

Mal is gripping the steering wheel such a death grip that I suddenly find myself worried about the state of his poor, white knuckles.

"Get out," Mal's whisper is a shout. "Just get the fuck out. I don't ever want to hear you talk about Flo. I knew that that was what this was about. Now get out."

Huh?

Who?

What now?

"What are you talking about?" He's parked in the middle of the road; the fact that we didn't get rear-ended is a miracle.

"You fucking know what I'm talking about," he growls, still grasping the steering wheel. "I know you do. Everybody knows. I'm the boy that can't let go. A walking wound. So what if my best friend killed herself? The whole fucking world thinks that I'm making this huge deal, as if I just want attention and to drag this misery out as long as fucking possible. I can't go home, I can't see my parents.

Pictures of her are everywhere, pictures of us as kids and I look at it and I still can't grasp why they had to give her death so much attention. Her life was special. She was the fucking best to be alive around and showing her dead body the way that they did? I mean, some of those fuckers zoomed in on it. When I complained about it, people told me that if she didn't want that to happen, she should have killed herself in private. How does someone say something like that?

That's what nobody seems to understand, they think that she killed herself for attention, but I know that's not why she did it. Flo hated attention. She fucking despised it; she used to get sick whenever she was centre of it," his words explode from within him, heavy and leaded. I try to sit back, eyeing his heaving chest.

His breathing has become dangerous.

"Our high school graduation was a gong show. Flo spent a good thirty minutes in the bathroom just freaking out. She thought nobody knew, but I totally knew. I made it my business to know, but when she finally came out, I just acted all cool. Like I didn't care, and I couldn't see the snot running down her nose. I knew she'd given herself a good thirty-minute freak out, trying to find a way out. She would have snuck out the back if I had helped her out. I should have helped her out."

His voice quickly becomes hollow. I feel terrible. I want to reach out. I'm scared he'll slap me though.

"I didn't know," I tell him, but I don't know if it's the truth. I didn't know, but I did somehow. Not all the blurry and fucked up details but I knew that Mal had lost someone he'd cared about. Or still cares about. I don't know.

"I'm sorry Mal," didn't I hate when people told me they were sorry about Alex? They never really meant it. They just didn't know what to say in my presence. I was a zombie. I looked like a drug addict hanging by a thread even though I never touched shit like that. I get drunk, but that's it. I'd like to think that I don't need it, but I know deep down that that's just utter bullshit. I do need it. I need the numbness and the silliness that follows taking that first sip. I need to laugh. I need to feel weightless. I just hate admitting that.

"Come on. Let's keep going to **Walmands**. You said it yourself you need food and I could use some socializing with strangers in a public forum. We can people watch while we shop, that's always fun, and we can keep talking if you want, or not." Either way I'm good.

Mal looked up. His eyes blank with a mixture of misery and shock. I stopped being afraid of him and leaning in to touch him, grazing my lips along his jaw while I longed to make us both senseless with kisses. I resisted and sat back, breathing the air around us in.

"Let's do this."

54 Say It Again - Mal

"Let's do this," she said. Cadence. Do what? Sit in my car causing a traffic jam? Staring each other into a shocked silence?

I can't believe I told her all of that. What the fuck is wrong with my head? I don't get it.

"What is your end game here Cadence?" I have to ask because her eyes are too bright, and her smile is haunted with too much of my own happiness. I've tasted it.

I don't get any of it.

"Fuck the rich boy? Is that it? Break my heart and get some laugh out of it? If that's your plan, I have some bad news. My heart is already broken; you can't re-break it. I'm not made of glass, but I'll still lay my shattered pieces in your bare hands. Do you want that?" I ask and watch as Cadence seems to think about it before shrugging and giving me her best impression of a careless and care free person.

"I don't know man. If you're into that kind of shit, I guess." I don't buy any of it. Not in the slightest.

"Fine," I'll happily call her bullshit on sight when I see it, "you want to go to **Walmands** and talk, let's do it."

I lift my foot off of the break and touch the gas with a gentle push that creates a sly grin on Cadence's face, like she just offered me some challenge and expected me to back away from it. But I didn't.

Yeah, let's do this. Can you tell that I'm sarcastic? I hope you can, because after that mid-afternoon sex I'm a little exhausted. I don't feel like putting much effort into it.

I looked back at the road as I got honked at by a soccer mom in a minivan. I flipped the soccer mom off and glared at Cadence when she laughed. I don't even think she noticed, she just continued to laugh. That made me mad.

Cadence was too easy to get along with. She was too easy to do everything with. I didn't like her for making me feel like that. I actually wanted to hate her for it.

I ground my jaw when we pulled up to **Walmands**. I parked as close as I could and hopped out, locking my door with the back of my hand and turning around to wait for Cadence. I made sure to grab a hoodie out of my trunk to cover up my top half; I didn't want to get banned from **Walmands** for heading in shirtless, although I'm sure that some of the hot cashiers would have loved it.

I know Cadence did.

She couldn't stop staring at my chest. I smirked and glanced down at her ass. My shirt barely covers it; that's why I asked her to wear it. I wouldn't be able to control myself if she were wearing that dress. At least with her in my shirt I stand somewhat of a chance. I laugh, and Cadence looks back. We've stepped up onto the sidewalk leading into **Walmands**, and I reach for her hand because it suddenly feels like a habit.

She has small hands. Her black nail polish is chipped. This doesn't settle well in my stomach.

"Why do you do that?" she whisper-asks. "One second you look like a smug asshole, the next you just look sad."

Because I'm human?

I don't have a much better response than that. The automatic doors open, I look up and for a second feign like I'm telekinetic, somehow magically pushing them back. No one laughs.

Walmands always has massive line ups, half empty shelves and a terrible left over selection. I keep a firm grip on Cadence and her tiny hand, keeping her tight against my hip.

I feel suddenly protective of her or some shit.

Don't question it.

55 Don't Break It - Cadence

I let Mal hold my hand. I should have questioned it, but instead I just fell into easy steps with him while looking around the supermarket otherwise known as **Walmands**. They sell clothes, electronics, housewares and they even have a domestics section. My favourite is the books department to be quite honest. Reading is awesome.

I want to stroll towards the romance section, but I don't want Mal to say anything sarcastic, so I stop myself from running ahead. For some reason, I feel like a little kid again. I don't want to wonder too far out of Mal's grasp, and frankly that doesn't make any fucking sense. I don't even know him.

I have no reason to feel better about myself while standing next to him. That's just sad. Most of the time I pride myself on not needing a man unless it's for sex, but something about this already feels different. We headed towards the grocery section. I eyed the plus sized clothing department and told Mal to go ahead, I'd surly follow him in a second. I hated shopping for clothes; I had never been any good at it. I headed straight for the clearance rack, feeling all sorts of self-conscious when I picked up a pair of size twenty-two pants, holding them out against my hips.

I hate looking at big people clothes in public. They always suck, the fabric clingy and thin and also pricey as shit. For some reason just because there's an extra five inches, the price has to double. People I've loved told me to diet, but I'm big boned.

I can't help the way my body is.

I look up when I hear a voice just to my left. A laughing and whispering group of bitches have perked up out of the bushes. I know that they have no business being in the big bitches' section.

"I don't think they should let fat people like that shop. What about the rest of us? Having to look at someone like that?"

Someone like what?

"She's so gross to look at. I mean look at those pants. How far can sweat pants really stretch? The poor fabric looks like it's going to start screaming for someone to rescue it." The leader of the bitch pack cackled into the back of her tiny hand. She had her nails done and I would be lying if I said that I wasn't the slightest bit jealous. I'd never been good at makeup and nails. Things like that went beyond my few talents. I mean, sure I could cake on a good pound of foundation but I looked the same with or without it: a tall, fat crappy piece of existence.

I'm ugly, outside and in. I've always felt like that.

"I can hear you," I said. That's all I said. I took the pair of pants I had taken off of the hanger and rack and quietly put them back. I started to move towards a display of grey sweatpants with red words on the ass, carefully aware of the bitch pack. I've always had a hard part in my heart for women who belittle other women. Even when I was a kid, the girls who tormented me seared themselves into my brain. I never forgot any of their names. If a boy got in my way, I smacked him until he learned his place, but boys are mean where girls are winning at cruelty. The pain is not the same.

"Hey, did you find something?" I was shocked to hear Mal's voice reaching to me. His hand is touching the space between my shoulder blades. I shrugged; I didn't need to buy anything. I had clothes at my place, lots of clothes. They may not have been nice, but they were mine, I bought them with the money saved.

"I'm fine," I lied, realizing a moment too late that Mal hadn't exactly asked if I was okay. The silence between us was booming.

Mal had found a cart somehow in my clothing fuelled haze. He had the bottom filled quite nicely: corn chips, toilet paper, water and an extra-large bucket of butter.

"Is that all you're getting? You can't even mix any of it together!" I observed, pointing a finger into his shopping cart. "Okay, maybe just maybe you could make some weird desert out of the corn chips and butter but I wouldn't want to eat it after."

I watched Mal smirk, momentarily glad that he didn't take my teasing to heart. I liked to shit disturb. I placed my hands on Mal's hips and walked behind him, I couldn't help myself as I glanced over my shoulder, looking for the bitchy girls. It felt so weird being here together, out in public. Shopping like a couple or friends or some other shit I didn't want to start. It was super fucking weird. To get back to the food side of the store where Mal had obviously lingered before, we had to pass by the cashiers. There weren't many of them working at this strange hour, not that it was even dark, but it was around most people's supper time.

I usually just ate small snacks through the day, nothing all that filling since I was never really all that hungry.

"What are you thinking?" Mal didn't stop walking or look back to talk to me; my hands left his waist and I tried not to be embarrassed for planting them there in the first place.

"Me? Oh, nothing. Just wondering why they don't put more girls on when they always have massive lines." I wasn't totally lying. That had kind of been what I'd been thinking, but only in a sort-of-not-really way.

I looked at the front windows that we could only just see as he walked by. It was still bright outside and for some reason I desperately wanted it to be raining.

Rain for some reason seems to mean peace and tranquility. Nothing bad ever happened while it was raining. Only good things, but all good things get washed away eventually.

The only thing permanent about life is a pain. I found that out the hard way, or the easy way I guess you could say. I pushed at my boundaries until they bounded back and slapped me in the face.

"You okay?" This time Mal did stop walking, I smiled but felt like I was grimacing.

"Great," I bullshitted so awkwardly.

I felt my chest break when he looked down and away, Mal was embarrassed by me. Duh. Obviously. Who wouldn't be embarrassed to be seen in public with a train wreck such as me? I mean really. I clicked my tongue while thinking, a bad habit I had never really been able to break. What was he doing here with me? I mean, really? I fucked him, I was easy (I want to add apparently into that, but we all know that isn't the case). Mal was using me.

56 Some Like It Hot - Mal

Caddie being disturbingly quiet bothered me. I couldn't quite place my finger on why, but her shy frown did something to my insides. I asked if she was okay for like the hundredth time, but she just kept smiling at me and for some reason, I imagined fangs instead of teeth.

Caddie looked kind of scary when she was angry, stewing over something that wouldn't jump out at me,

I had done something wrong apparently.

"Are all you girls the same? I mean I don't blink right and suddenly it's like World War III only you're giving me the silent treatment and without you talking, I feel like I'm being hammered by a hundred grenades." I was speaking without meaning.

Caddie looked at me out of the corner of her eye.

"I didn't do anything. Don't be mad at me," she all but squeaked and this made me laugh harder than almost anything.

She couldn't even pretend to be scared of me, and I smiled unhelpfully. This girl didn't play the damsel easily.

"I don't know what you're doing to me," I told her honestly. "You make me happy, and it's such a weird feeling. Mostly because it's not so much happiness as it is looking forward to something. You're so quick to bite me that I can't help but want to make you angry or annoyed, but please tell me. Whatever did I do this time?" I was referring to the way she sighed after looking outside, becoming shy suddenly. I didn't like her pretending to be shy or mousy around me.

"You're using me," she whispered, grabbing my attention suddenly. We were in the produce section, and I stopped so suddenly I rammed my shopping cart into the ass of an old lady. She was bending down to look closer at a display. Her husband grumbled something at me. I wasn't listening.

"I'm not using you Caddie," I told the truth stupidly and easily. I liked the idea of her being cross with me, but the idea of her hurting because of me was like being stabbed in the side. No fucking way.

"You showed up at my place and came onto me. You inserted yourself into my life without asking." I took what you were offering. I shut my mouth and closed my eyes, breathing her fire into me.

She's crossed her arms. She's pouting. In front of my oranges and apples. Seriously.

I'd never known a girl who could look semi-cute while pouting without making me angry. Most of the time when girls pouted it just annoyed me. I hated being pegged as the big bad guy, as if I had done something horrific if I didn't blend to their way of thinking.

We stopped shopping in amongst the fruits and veggies and headed towards the meats. I hadn't cooked anything as of late. Ordering in or going out for food was just as easy but hardly ever cheap. My money train was slowing. I refused to borrow or beg. That just wasn't my thing.

"Are you going to ask anything?" I directed my question at Caddie, slowing so that she could walk right beside me instead of behind me, although her hands on my hips intrigued me.

She kept finding excuses to touch me, sighing quietly whenever her skin brushed mine. I shared the strange relief. As if some big weight had settled on my chest but when Caddie touched me I felt like I could finally breathe. It was terrifying, addicting, strange, new and fascinating.

She still hadn't answered me about wanting to get anything. Her side of my cart is empty. I peer down into the mess of groceries. I know that she has a place she must stay, as she never said anything about needing to stay with me. I wonder if the place she's staying is safe.

I don't know why this bothers me.

"Hello? Earth to Caddie?" Her attention snaps back to me; she'd been picking at the skin of her lip quite violently.

"Do you want me to take you home after?" Or you could just come with me? "I know you probably don't want to come back to my place. I'm just going to unpack all this shit and go to sleep. Maybe finish cleaning?" Please come back to my place.

Should I feel guilty for wanting such a thing? I want to feel guilty.

I can't think about the reason without completely breaking so I just push it to the brink of my memories. Everything is easier that way, walking around not quite numb, but somewhat empty.

My heart wasn't breaking because it had been broken already. Everything good in me had already ceased to be, *until Caddie.*

Yeah, that wasn't something I was willing to scream or even admit to myself in the dark of night, let alone in the light of day.

I kept walking.

"My car is at your place." Cadence's voice is sullen but not weak; I want to look deep into her eyes and see if they're heavy with anything or everything that she keeps buried.

Talk to me, I want to keep saying, but I know the best thing to do sometimes is not say anything. I make a U-turn through the deli and head back towards the tills to pay, pulling into a line of crying toddlers and pissed off looking old ladies. I take a moment to get a good look at everyone around me. **Walmands** is not a classy place by any means. No one dresses up before shopping, they dress down if anything.

The woman in front of me is wearing leggings and forgot to put on underwear obviously. She's not bad looking, but her curves are not mouth-watering, only distracting in the worst way, with the worst parts of her on full display. I know that someone could probably say the same thing about me.

"I know what you're doing," says Caddie, whispering those sweet words teasingly as she stands on her tip toes to reach me. The difference in our heights is only made obvious when we're both standing upright. I grin mischievously before my brain can sucker punch me.

"You're eye-judging that lady and I don't appreciate it. Seriously Mal, people can see you and if you have a problem with big people wearing tight clothes you might want to glance down at the company you've dragged along with you. I wear tight clothes, and I would curl up on in on myself if I were being looked at the way you're looking at that poor woman right now."

Her words are true. I can't help myself.

"I like when you wear tight clothes though. You look hot as hell in spandex, especially my spandex and if I ever catch you wearing something loose fitting, I'll rip it at the seams. Understand me? I'm not judging anybody." I wasn't lying, and I was maybe. Straight through my perfect teeth.

I was cocky and proud of my body. It was one of the things that she always hated most about me. She being the center of my being. I breathed in deeply as the pain overtook me, looking down at my sad groceries.

"Let's go." I heard myself say. "I don't have time to stand in line all day; I'll drop you off at your place. You can come get your car later or tomorrow. There's somewhere I've got be."

There wasn't really.

57 Trust Me, Please? - Cadence

He left me at my place. I gave him directions, but he stayed quiet the entire way. This got to me.

"Did I do something?" I almost screeched when Mal slammed on the breaks, reaching past me to unlock my door and push it open for me. He was trying to get rid of me. He fucked me, used me. Ran me dry and screamed at me and now he was dumping me.

Great.

Thanks.

All in the span of like a day. Jesus Christ.

"What? No, I just need some head-space. I need to think. I'll call or something," he lied. I never gave him my number, and he had never asked. He asked for my address and I rattled it off to him.

He asked out of convenience. That was it. I wanted there to be more to it but there wasn't. Not in the slightest. What the fuck was going on in my head? I couldn't grasp the thoughts and feelings that all felt foreign.

I felt like my head and my heart, had been invaded by aliens. I grunted and got out, slamming the door shut behind me and hating his low riding car, getting out of it was never pretty.

"Fuck you Malachi!" I screamed as loudly as I could through clenched teeth. I still felt like my heart was breaking when he sped away from me.

My door was locked, and I didn't have my keys or my purse or anything that could be of use to me.

I banged on the door and screamed for Torrance to get his ass out of bed and let me in already. He wasn't home apparently.

"Fucking seriously?" I hit the door again just for good luck and turned on my heels, looking out into my parking lot. I could break in, but I didn't have any tools for that. I also didn't want to get arrested if one of my neighbours saw and decided to call the cops.

Knowing my luck, that would totally happen.

I stood on my front steps for half a minute and just contemplated my sad and pathetic existence. I was a complete and total loser at twenty-seven, how had this happened? How had I let it?

I knew that I didn't want to do anything about it simply because I wouldn't, but I still wanted to hate on myself because of it. I am after all, a woman. Don't we all do this? Find every flaw on our own retched skin and magnify it? I was used to doing this; I almost took comfort in it.

I decided to head around back; I could break into one of the back windows without getting noticed. I was almost sure of it. I wasn't the best at maintaining the yard or the garden, and neither was Torrance, so it was a mess to step through. I was only wearing my flip-flops, and they kept coming off. I had to pause to readjust them.

Mal's shirt got hung up on a branch whenever I dared to stop. I tried to keep a leash on my frustration. It wouldn't do me any good to have a hissy fit in public. I rolled my eyes and tilted my head back, shielding the sun out of my vision with my hand. From this viewpoint, our place looked massive. An impenetrable prison even though I knew it wasn't.

I tried the back door first just because I'm not a total idiot, but stopped cold and dead when it slowly pushed open.

It wasn't locked.

This was a hell of a shock.

I called again for Torrance just because but when he didn't respond I knew he was off doing whatnot. He never left anything unlocked; he was a super strict asshole about it more often than not. I was always the one to forget, only to be screamed at.

I wish I knew what Torrance was so afraid of. For such a big guy, you'd think he wouldn't be in fear of much but he obviously was. "Hello? Is anyone here? I've got a baseball bat and a knife." I didn't, but they didn't need to know that. I walked in and kicked my shoes off, closing the door behind me and locking it. I walked straight forward into the kitchen to make myself a snack but was dumbfounded by the scent that seemed creased into every corner of it.

Death and sadness. Both permanent.

I blinked and looked around, covering my mouth and nose with my hands. The floor wasn't exactly spotless, but it still wasn't a mess. The counters had numerous piles of crap spread out over them. This was normal; I was used to my place looking like this. What I wasn't used to was the flash that blinded me for half a second. Green and black, a painting of misery and blackness. A paintbrush smearing on a blank canvas. I saw my death. All of it. I saw myself getting wasted and covering myself in vomit when I puked. I was alone in my kitchen, half naked. The top of my dress had come undone by unclean hands, and I was now a dirty angel on the linoleum.

I blinked again and stepped back.

The floor was halfway clean again and the smell of rotting flesh no longer as persistent. I couldn't believe what I had just witnessed, or imagined. I couldn't find the difference between the two. I felt like I was going to be sick all over again.

"Cadence?" I turned at the sound of my name being said, but it wasn't a man who said or groaned it. I was used to that.

It was just nothingness.

58 Patience - Mal

I headed to my once favourite spot, the spot that I now hated. I drove there going way beyond the legal limit. Darkness was setting in, and I almost laughed, it was a Saturday night, and this was how I was choosing to spend it.: alone in my Chevy™ racing into madness. Directly into it.

Buffalo Falls isn't a grand tourist attraction. It never has been, but the recent events of its past had tried to change that. Thank God they didn't, turns out most people were still halfway decent.

I drove straight for it even though I wanted to stop and have a piss. I didn't, I just held it. Blasting the radio before getting sick of it, I reached over in to my glove compartment, searching for music and silence and the best of both of it.

I finally settled on a CD by *Deciding darkness* Flo loved this kind of shit, and I loved her for it. I skipped ahead to track seven, a song titled *Breakfast* and just listened to the beauty of it.

The next song was called *in my head* I let my mind sink into the abyss of blackness it always carried with it.

Inside of my head you live/we have no time to go over this.

What was it I felt for Cadence? I couldn't understand, but I knew for some reason that it had something to do with the grief battling its way into my chest. I already had a home for it.

I almost welcomed it. The highway felt deserted, but I knew that it wasn't, cars passed me in blurs, but I failed to notice. My ears were only attuned to the music. My hands had started to twitch.

Cadence fits into the darkness. That was the only thought in my head that seemed to make sense, even though I couldn't fathom my meaning behind it. I saw the green sign glowing up again.

Buffalo Falls, next exit.

I signalled and headed straight for it.

59 Wait for It - Cadence

I showered and got dressed, pulling on a pair of soft shorts and a tank top, and one of my favourite thin baby blue t-shirts over it. I looked into the bathroom mirror, seeking my reflection.

My hair was still a mess, but I liked the bravery that I felt edging from every strand. I pushed the excess skin on my neck back, tilting my head and searching for bruises that I knew no longer existed.

Mal didn't have a heavy and violent hand but most men that I had been with had. They used strength to pin point my weaknesses. I had tons of them. My body was mistake ridden.

I shook my shoulders and breathed my energy in. I could do this, I could stand up straight and strong and pretend like I deserved to do exactly that, even though I knew that I didn't.

I left my bathroom light on and headed into the kitchen again. I grabbed a diet sprite and went into the living room to have a nap. I sat on the couch, but it was only a minute before I ended up on my back, again.

I stared at the ceiling and tried to find meaning in it–a hidden pattern, something special and unique to the thoughts in my head.

Nothing happened.

I wanted to talk to someone. I wanted to talk to Torrance, and I wanted to talk to Alex. I wanted to call my parents, but I knew by glancing at the clock that it was too late for that. I rolled over onto my stomach and reached for the house phone we kept plugged into the living room for some strange reason. It's not like we needed it, we each had cell phones and a computer to **Facestory** message for help if needed it.

I picked up the receiver and started dialing a number without understanding how I knew it, I just did. I felt like I had dialed it a hundred times in the last twenty minutes. It rang and rang, and I let it. His voice is clipping on the other end as he told me to leave a message.

I didn't. Instead, I hung up and tried and tried again. I got nothing but his voice and the gnawing pit in my stomach.

I kept calling him. I couldn't help it. I knew that this made me look psychotic, but I didn't give a shit. I just needed to talk to him; I needed to know where he was headed. I needed to understand everything he was trying too hard to keep hidden. I needed to understand him and for some reason I felt like I already did. The fiftieth time his voice clipped I did leave a message. Again, I simply couldn't help it. I just wanted him to hear it.

"Hey Mal, it's Cadence. I know this seems awkward, and I swear I didn't look up your phone number, I just knew it. I don't know how I knew it, but that isn't the point of this very one-sided conversation." I took a deep breath in and started to play with my spare hand.

"I can't stop thinking about your kiss. I felt alive when my lips touched your lips, and I felt happiness and depression and warmness. I felt whole for half a minute and I want to do it again. There's some things we're going to talk about if we're going to be friends, but frankly I'd understand if you didn't want to be even that. I know you're probably freaked out by all of it, but I love..." I love you, man, I almost said, but I stopped myself before that could happen. I couldn't love Mal, I hardly knew him and yet I felt like I did for some strange reason. "Anyway, call me when and if you get this." I hung up and felt like a total idiot. I can't believe that I just did that.

And yet I did.

I have officially lost it.

60 Accept It - Mal

I don't know what I had expected this place to give, but nothingness just wasn't it. I couldn't even see the bottom in the darkness, but I knew that later my heart would thank me for this.

I didn't want to see how far my best friend had fallen, but I already had. I knew that I wouldn't be able to stand a fresh image. Memories are easier to subside when they are less vibrant.

I know this.

I leave Buffalo Falls the way I found it. With an empty head and a thousand unanswered questions. My chest ached with every movement, but I did my best to ignore it. It felt like forever since I had done this, just gravelled in my loneliness, totally ready to drown in it.

It was a relief to stop fighting it for half a second. I let it in, I accepted it.

My life was utter shit.

It hadn't always been, but lately I just looked around and saw only that which was meaningless: school, my place, my reflection.

My thoughts didn't just suddenly turn to Cadence because they had never let her begin with. She was every star in my sad imagination. She was the water and the wind, and I didn't fucking understand it.

There was no loss when she was touching me, skin on skin. We had barely even done anything, and I wanted to do it again. When she kissed me, it was like all the shit had never happened, as if the loss of my best friend was just a nightmare I couldn't get out of my head. The way I felt around Cadence wasn't new, but I wasn't used to feeling it. The only other person who had ever made me feel like that was dead.

61 Pray for It - Cadence

I woke up to a pounding that for once wasn't in my head, I was still on the couch. Still on my stomach. I had no idea what time it was, but I got up just for the hell of it. "What do you want?" I called as the pounding stopped and started once again. I knew it was coming from the front door, but I headed to the back because I was simply a chicken shit.

I touched the lock and turned around again, the sound of a man breathing was persistent and desperate. Unforgiving at its finest.

I knew who was at the door before I even found the courage to open it. When I finally did open it, I felt my heart shatter in my chest. Mal looked back at me with sadness in his eyes, but his body felt like the humming of an engine. He rushed towards me with his eager grasp, and I sunk right into it like an idiot.

My chest touching his, I tilted my head back and kissed him. Our kisses are suddenly filled with longing and tasting of innocence. I reached for his shirt and pulled it over his head. Looking at his bare chest and marvelling at the deliciousness of it. His skin was perfect, strong.

He formed my ideal safety net.

I backed up out of the kitchen and felt Mal's hands sliding down past my ass. He pushed my shorts down, and I stepped out of them, his hands making quick use of my shirt. He disposed of it.

I kept walking backwards. I was not afraid to trip, I knew he would catch me if I did.

"You should fight me." He said against my lips. I was already breathless, but I kissed him again just for the hell of it. I was now completely naked, and he was still wearing pants. "You should tell me that we shouldn't do this." I knew he didn't mean it but for some reason I think it makes him feel better to say it. I knew he wasn't trying to make me feel bad for being easy for him. He was giving me the chance to get away from him, but I wasn't about to take it. Not a chance.

We backed into my bedroom, and I pushed the door open with my hip, leaving the light off. I felt myself stepping around a mess of clothing and books that I had long ago read.

My bed found us as we tumbled on top of it, a mess of moaning and tangled limbs. Mal rid himself of his pants, holding himself above me with both hands. I felt safe. I felt guarded. I felt noticed.

He kissed me again, and I knew that there wasn't any need for words even if I could make myself find them again. I couldn't speak; I couldn't do anything but touch him. I opened up to him in a way that made me feel like I had never been with any other man before him. All that mattered was this, and I was totally one-hundred-percent okay with that.

At least for this second, I hoped this would last until my death.

Mal's hands found my hips as his lips left my chin, finding my neck and my breasts. He chewed on my skin. Licking it and tasting it. I arched my back, waiting for him to fill me and he did.

It felt like heaven. Moving as one with him. He grabbed my hair and pulled it and slapped my sweaty skin.

I felt reddened. I felt exhausted and when he finally dropped onto my chest, skin against skin, only caving in once we had both been pushed to our limits. I reached out to touch his chin. I pushed his dark hair back. I loved him.

I don't know how I knew it but I did. I felt like I had always loved him; he was just a part of my history that had been blocked out of my existence until I was ready for it. Until I deserved it.

I wanted so badly to tell him, but I was terrified of him leaving and never coming back to me again. He looked so handsome. Asleep on my chest, an angel, and a gigantic one at that.

I couldn't help but laugh.

Mal stirred, and I automatically felt bad for waking him.

Crap.

"What was that?" he moved and almost hit me in the nose with his forehead, I pulled away for half a second, readying myself for a blast of aggression that never hit. Mal didn't even have his eyes open.

"What was what?" I asked.

He smiled, and I touched his lips with my hand, tracing the look of happiness on him. It made my own heart swell with hunger and regret–a regret I couldn't pinpoint or understand.

"You laughed," he smiled again. God dammit my heart just couldn't take it. "I liked the sound of it. Scratch that, I loved the sound of it. Do it again Cadence." He demanded and the sound of my name on his lips didn't make me laugh. It made me do the opposite.

I lifted my head and kissed him.

He held back for half a second before moving his arms to either side of my head, caging me in once again.

I lifted my legs around his waist and felt alive when he thrust into me again, solid and strong. He had a strength that could ruin anyone who neared it as he powered into my body, taking all of my sense with him.

I thought only this. I would give anything to feel this way again and again. I never wanted to lose him or it. The price of emotions is rising the more that I thought about it. What wouldn't I do for this? I was almost afraid to ask.

62 My Last Breath - Mal

I woke up on top of Cadence. Still buried deep within her warmth, I was almost embarrassed. Surely I hadn't fallen asleep in the middle of all of sex? Her smile told me that no, I hadn't.

"Good morning, sleepy head," she said with a soft kiss to my forehead. I lifted a hand to the flesh of her chest. Giving her left tit a little smack, she flinched before I kissed the reddened skin. Glancing up at her expression, she looked happy, glad, and I wanted to know the reasoning behind it. I wanted a way to define what we just did. Over and again.

It felt like more than just sex. I knew that it had to be more than just sex. I felt it in every sense. I so desperately wanted to make sense of it, but I was worried asking about it would just ruin the moment.

Could I risk it?

"Whatever you want to say just say it," urged Cadence. Her voice was still soft, her face still seeming to radiate peacefulness.

"I don't know what happened," I said before I could talk myself out of it, Cadence opened her mouth to laugh, but I jumped up and silenced her with a quick kiss, "don't laugh, I am well aware that we just had earth shattering and mind blowing sex but what I mean, and yes I am about to be a total bitch about this, but what does it mean? What did it mean for you and us?" God I hated saying that. Us.

The two of us as a couple was a terrifying thought, and I hated myself for admitting that but I couldn't help it. Everything was just so sudden. It freaked me out a wee bit. God.

I had turned into a total bitch. I pulled the blanket up around Cadence so that she wasn't cold or embarrassed to be with me like this. So naked, it was probably a stupid concern but I still felt it.

I looked up at Cadence again, afraid of what I would feel if she was looking at me like I was an idiot, a strong man turned into a door mat. But she didn't. She touched my chin and sighed again.

"We're friends," she simply said. "I mean that's something isn't it? Let's be friends and see what happens." She shrugged, and I immediately felt my stomach twist. Well, that was like being drop kicked onto a mountain made of cement and pricks. I couldn't help but flinch.

Well then...I peeled myself off of her salty skin and pushed back the blankets so that I could free my feet and stand. She didn't try to grab for my hands and this also was like being repeatedly sucker punched in the stomach. It shouldn't have been.

I'd had one night stands, dozens of them. But this felt different. Everything with Cadence had felt different since the second she forced her way into my kitchen. I felt like I had known her my whole life rather than five minutes. I felt a comfort in her presence that slipped under my skin and soaked in. She was sunlight drenched in darkness but for some reason, I was all in.

Too bad Cadence wasn't. Once I was out of the bed, I breathed calmly in and started looking for my pants. I bent over to look under the bed, and it made Cadence laugh again.

Fuck I loved the sound of that.

"You have a nice ass man, it's like firm and adorable but still tough, you know? Not many guys have an ass that looks like it could kick another ass's... well ass." She grinned into the back of her hand, turning on her side as she watched me scour through her mess of crap. Her bedroom was covered in everything a woman could ever purchase.

Most of it was tucked away into corners, but I could still see most of it. Her dresser looked like it was stuffed full, panties and bras spilling over the edges. I found my pants, pulling them up and over my dick.

Cadence was still watching me when I found a man's jacket that I knew I hadn't showed up with.

Fuck. My brain swarmed by how many dudes had been in her bedroom before I had, if my dick wasn't already dead those thoughts made it limp. I wanted to go home and have a nap. I tried not to look at her as she said something in a soft whisper. I didn't want to care anymore. I started towards her bedroom door.

"Where are you going?" her soft voice carried in such a way I hadn't yet heard. She sounded small and scared. I suddenly turned and realized what I was doing had upset her. She had been talking to me, laughing and here I was, getting up and getting out without so much as a "see you later alligator." Sometimes my idiocy burned.

"You said that we're friends, but I don't want to be friends. I'm not going to be some guy you fuck on the side whenever you feel like it. I know we're moving a little quickly, but I don't have time to wait around anymore. Whatever this is, wherever you came from I wanted to make it work. I wanted to get to know each other up close and personal without a trial stage first. I was all in without any question marks, but you just putting all that down, well that hurt. I've had enough hurt, and I carry it every which way that my body works. I don't need fresh scars."

Her face didn't crumble and fill with tears, reminding me of another reason I liked her. She kept herself together, for the most part, I never felt like she was a step away from crying in my arms. I liked girls who could deal with the world with cold fingers, especially if those ice fingers had also melted my heart.

"I've never had a guy say shit like that to me before," she whispered, looking at her floor. I had my hands on my hips, but I moved towards her, bending down to brush back the front part of her hair. On her the look totally worked. She looked hard core. It made my dick hard.

I couldn't help but kiss her. Pulling away to intertwine my hands with hers, she had my whole heart, and I didn't even know her, and yet I knew somehow that this would work. Almost immediately I wanted us to move in together. I didn't care if it was a rushed start.

Taking our time wouldn't save our hearts. Or lock down a decent future. We had now. That's all that mattered.

"Move in with me," I told her. "I know you have some reason for living here but whatever it is, you can still do it from my place. I promise you, I won't stand in your way on anything unless it puts you in danger. I just want to know that you're safe in my arms. If that's too much for me to ask you, I don't know what we're doing here."

I tried to stare unapologetically down at her but the way her lips quivered almost killed my nerve. I didn't want to frighten her.

I also didn't want to lose her. For some reason I felt like this would hurt not worse than everything that had hurt me before, but as if it would be the final pull, tugging me away from her forever.

The exact *her* that I was referring too didn't matter.

All I saw was Cadence when I looked at her, but my heart told me a million different things better and worse. She felt like her. Different and like I said, better and worse.

"Say something baby because I'm dying over here." I knelt down in front of her, slowly kissing each finger. I use my best puppy dog eyes to try to sway her. She hadn't said a word.

"Mal I don't know what you want me to say. I mean I can't move in with you I live here, I need to look after..." she swallowed the words, holding in all the air before blowing it out into the atmosphere.

I kissed her hard. Harder and harder, climbing back on top of her when she moaned a slew full of words that mattered but I didn't care.

She said my name. I heard that part.

I pushed the blankets back until her naked chest was rubbing against my shirt, finding her and filling her until we had worked out all the words and found what truly mattered: our hearts, beating together as she screamed when I fucked her harder. Upside down and sideways. Face to face and face to hair. It didn't matter. All I wanted was her.

63 Can We Start Over? - Cadence

I had woken up a hundred different times in his arms before the day was over. Every time I would roll over and kiss him until we shivered and rid our bodies of the sheets and covers.

I was full and tired and overworked, but I felt like I could still party until even my brain hurt. Mal's finger slowly moved downwards, springing me to life once more. He kissed my shoulder and smiled into my hair. "You smell like a rainstorm," he muttered. "That's how I know that you're here, that this could be forever."

Forever.

I guess that's a start.

Epilogue and Forever

This Is What Matters - Flo

I feel better. I feel better because I know that my best friend no longer feels worse. I'm still here, somewhere.

A distant star in the atmosphere or a whisper when Mal brushes back her hair. I am a part of Cadence because I felt her heart. I'm not quite as jealous as I was before, although it still hurts. I know that Cadence needed a safe harbour. Now Mal is hers.

They grow together. Laugh together and love together even when they fall apart. I love her like a sister. I want to love her like a sister. That's how close I feel to her. Like a piece of my own heart that someone broke but sewed back together. When I look at myself in a mirror I kind of see her.

So yes, I feel better. I feel worse. Our story still matters. Our love is like the stars, always there but only visible in the dark. I felt her pain; I felt her dying on her kitchen floor as my entire world was pulled apart. I wanted her to get a second chance, I wanted to live through her. I was selfish, her heart was pure. Our love is like a star.

I'm still here, but I don't want to be here anymore. I still don't feel like this is fair, Mal. Don't leave me here, at least not for forever.

Mal?

Hello?

Are you still there? Oh whatever. I stomp my feet and dance in a circle. I'm nowhere and everywhere. I can't touch anything. I can still see and hear. I'm still all over what is now hers.

I'm the former owner.

The rejected loser.

I really am stuck here.

I hear Cadence's own words.

Forever.

Stay tuned for a preview of the continuation of Ache for You, with the next book in the series:

Trapped in Three Hill, Book # 2

Anything for You

Synopsis

For Torrance and Emelia, nothing has ever been simple. From the outside in, with his light gaze and blonde surfer hair, Torrance looks like the golden boy with everything he could ever want in the world.

Unfortunately, at twenty-four years old, nothing could be further from the truth.

Years of heartache and loss have made him rude, closed off. His heart is ice cold. The only person he's close to is twenty-nine-year-old train wreck Cadence Smalls, the sister of his dead best friend. With her gone off with her new, cougar bait boyfriend Mal, Torrance becomes even more cut off and alone. It will take a miracle to reach him now.

For Emelia Winters, she never planned to be the kind of girl who could simply vanish off the face of the earth at only nineteen years old. The daughter of the mayor of Three Hill and his alcoholic wife, Deliria. Emelia has never gone unnoticed, until now.

Her life has always looked spotless, the cracks covered with paint and the bruises fading too quickly for any outsider to see. Two-and-half years after her disappearance, something big and untouchable will bring Torrance and Emelia, two strangers, together.

Torrance doesn't believe in fate. He hates the word and the idea of ghosts is purely absurd. Emelia opens her big blue eyes to a world that moved happily along without her. Will she be able to understand, and figure out what happened to her?

Can fantasy and a pull unlike any other truly bring two completely different people together? Torrance and Emelia would do absolutely anything for one another. Life is hard, but living alone without the person you are meant for is a lot harder.

TRAPPED IN THREE HILL,
BOOK # 2

ANYTHING FOR YOU

NANCY BEAUDET

Prologue

Nice to Meet You Dude - Emelia

I only planned on disappearing for a short while, I just wanted to vanish. I wanted to be my own ghost.

The beautiful blue eyed, dark haired angel that everybody used to know, the so called *good-girl.* I had always been small, even at nineteen years old I was petite and could have easily been mistaken for a child.

I wasn't weak though, I refused to be picked up or moved unless I wanted to move myself. You could not make me do anything that I didn't want to do. It just wasn't possible.

My name was Emelia Isabelle Winters, I was nineteen-years-old two and a half years ago when I vanished down a beautiful back road. I packed my beloved pick up truck full of everything that I had ever owned, all of the things that I still needed and I wanted to keep close.

My blue striped pick up truck wasn't fancy, or clean. Internally or externally, the sides were muddy. It was built in the early 1990's.

There was a CD player I had installed; a necessity no real human can do without. We don't have any cool radio stations in Three Hill.

The windows and door locks were manual so whenever I felt vaguely creeped out, I would lean across the front bench seat and push the locks down. It was October now and the weather outside was beautiful. I had decided to cut my thick hair all on my own. I used an army knife, cutting awkwardly. The green and yellow trees fading into grass that was quickly turning gold, where it wasn't already covered in snow.

I had a backpack full of my favourite clothes, hoodies and leggings. I was wearing my favourite pink and brown cowboy boots.

My dark hair now cut to shoulder length was hidden under a baseball cap. My blue jeans had holes in the knees. It was early on a Monday morning and the fresh air that time of day was always freezing. The hood of my truck was covered in frost from the previous night so I turned on defrost and cranked the heat.

The ice on my window was melting.

This was my way out, I hadn't told anyone where it was that I had planned to go, or that I was leaving at all. I kept it to myself mostly because I didn't have it all mapped out.

I just knew that I wanted out.

I felt like there was more waiting for me outside of Three Hill. Something undeniable and real. Three Hill was my home town and the town where my parents had moved with me when I was super little. Still drinking out of a bottle and drooling on myself.

I had grown up as an only child.

My father was the mayor of Three Hill, we had the biggest house on the tallest hill which overlooked the entire town. The fortress itself was hallow and cold, but isn't that always the way it goes?

This isn't a story about a poor rich girl, drawn to the wrong side of the tracks and a boy hidden in the shadows. The boy I wanted and loved, was beautiful, and built of gold. Torrance Clearwater had been his name, and he had glowed. He had no idea who I was though, we were separated by a few years so we never had any classes together in school.

I saw him one day from the opposite side of the hall, he was tall, probably about six foot two.

His natural blonde locks resting against a strong jaw that made him look ruggedly handsome. His pale blue eyes would sometimes sadden, as if the light he carried had sudden been extinguished. He would flex the muscle in his arms as he stood, quietly frustrated.

He had obviously been glaring at someone or something that wasn't present. He would seem lost in his memory and in faded moments. I wanted to save him. The longing to know him was undeniable, but I ignored it anyhow. Pushing the feeling down.

Numbing myself. I would see him all the time after graduating from Three Hill high school, I would see him around town. I even saw him at the park, sitting by himself on the ground. He would be watching the soft water of the lake, seemingly waiting for it to come in and go back out, even though it never moved.

Torrance Eliot Clearwater looked damaged, but indestructible. Even though I don't think that those two things, together, are at all possible.

I really don't think so.

I only knew his middle and last name because I used to stalk his graduation photo that hung in the halls of our old high school. I thought about him when I decided to leave town.

I couldn't help myself.

I shifted into drive and started to coast, I had chosen this road because I knew how often it went unused.

It was an old gravel road, connected and hidden behind the only known way in and out of Three Hill. The most tended too road was the one most known about, this one on the other hand was full of pot holes.

I clenched the steering wheel, careful to keep my hands at ten and two. I breathed in and out, trying to calm myself.

I only planned on disappearing for a short while, I just wanted to vanish. I wanted to be my own ghost. The beautiful blue eyed, dark haired angel that everybody used to know.

I drove and thought to myself, that one day, when I was ready, I would just, I don't know, come home?

I didn't think it would be a big deal. I thought the world would figure out that I vanished under my own free will. I didn't think anyone would look for me, or that I wanted them too.

I didn't know.

One

Moments of Getting to Know You - Torrance

The world doesn't move on the way you want it to after you lose the one person who means everything to you. I sit alone in the dark waiting for you to come home. It's been nine years now, and it still doesn't feel real. Nine years since I was in that mini van with you. You swerved just a little, the headlights coming at us were all too predictable.

You died Alexander Smalls, but you didn't die alone. Your sister and I were with you. She was drunk and stoned, traumatized and crying into the carpet in the back, where all of the seats had been pushed down. She was curled into a ball.

How did she survive? She wasn't even wearing a seatbelt.

Why didn't do you live to tell the awful tale? You, Alexander Smalls, were wearing a seatbelt. You were driving us down the busy, dark two lane road. You invited me onto a rescue mission.

Your sister had gotten herself into trouble.

Didn't she always though?

We've spent nine years without you now. How has it been nine years now? The time goes by so fast, yet so slow when you sit and think about it all. You were only a child at sixteen years old.

You were my best friend Alexander Smalls and I miss you. Every single day I miss you, your fucked up sister is mine to worry about, but no longer mine to rescue. She went and got herself a fucked up boyfriend, isn't that just swell?

I really am alone now.

I sit in the park, drinking even though the warm sun went down hours ago. I rest my arms on my knees and look out at the lake. The water doesn't move, it actually kind of smells awful. Even though I'm not sitting all that close. The park is a refuge for homeless people.

The lake has become a dumping ground where they go to the bathroom, I wrinkle my nose taking another sip from my empty beer bottle. I'm tired, and cold. I just want to go home.

I can't though, because I know that the two-bedroom apartment I moved into with Cadence several years go, will be dark and cold.

She has all but officially, moved out. I toss my empty beer bottle and It rolls around the soft, grassy ground. Cadence lives with her boyfriend now, somehow, even though they argue and break up every other day or so. He always calls after it all, and she goes home.

It makes my blood boil.

I push myself up and stumble a little. I burst out laughing at myself. No one in Three Hill was surprised by my downfall. I'm sure that they could see it coming for miles, I lost myself when I lost you and you are not even officially dead and buried at all.

You're alone and immobile in a hospital room. Hooked up to breathing machines and tubes. Kept alive by technology even though your brain stopped working nine years ago.

You are dead, but they won't let you go.

I miss you but I can't see you. It hurts too much. This is sad and pathetic and selfish, I know. I just can't find the strength in me to go into that room and see you, on a bed. As white as a ghost, you're being fed through feeding tubes. You are obviously unwell.

I miss you.

Why can't you just wake up now?

Made in the USA
Charleston, SC
17 March 2016